THE TOMB

THE WATCHERS BOOK 1

CARL NOVAKOVICH

For Carl J. Bonavolanto, Jr. — Husband, Father, Grandfather, Great-Grandfather
And for all those we lost as a result of this horrible virus.
We will never forget you.

A MESSAGE_

PLEASE STOP WHAT YOU'RE DOING. LOOK AROUND you. Wherever you are in this moment, please pay close attention. Your neighbors, the people that might be walking by, your spouse — are they who you think they are? I ask you this because what I'm about to tell you will open your eyes to the truth of the world. As you continue, you will not be able to unsee the truth. However, I beg you to not stop reading because the world has already changed, but I guarantee that you have yet to see why. Not just for the people involved in this story, but for you as well.

This is not my story; I'm just helping it along. In fact, this is not a story at all. I'll be chiming in from time to time, as well as a couple friends of mine, to tell you the rest. Understand that what you are about to hear will change your life forever. Just know, everything you read will reflect your everyday life. It will open your eyes to the truth that has been around you this entire time.

Please, understand that what I am about to tell you is not something you should take lightly. So, please, read carefully, pay close attention, and most importantly — stay safe...

THE CASE_
JOHN

DECEMBER 2018
Chicago

Walking back from yet another food run. I feel like that is most of my job now. Walter Finch, my partner in the Chicago Police Department, sends me on quite a few of these. This is the same man who raised me after my aunt, who was like a mother to me, died. He was once in great shape, just like I am now, but he let himself go as the years got the best of him. After sixty years on this Earth, I guess it's easy to not care as much about the way you look. That, and he isn't the detective he once was — that might be my fault in a way. Now it's just, 'hey, John, how about a snack,' or 'hey, John, how about a sub?' The problem is, he usually considers a sub the same thing as a snack... the fat bastard.

Oh, and that's me, by the way — John Gideon. I'm half Walter's age. At just thirty, I still take care of the way I look. The way I see it, if I want to catch the criminals we're chasing, then I need to be in the best shape possible. Walter doesn't share the same ideals as I do. Hell, the day I joined the homicide and missing persons unit and became his partner was the day he officially checked out and had me complete all of his work. It's okay though, it's the least I can do for the man who was always there for me. He is the only family I have left. It would be nice to have him a bit more active in some cases, though.

I mean, for instance, today we are on a stake-out looking for a suspect that could be involved in a string of missing person cases we've been working on for over a year now. With thirteen people missing, four dead and, as of today, only one lead, I need all the help I can get. Unfortunately, Walter has only wanted to help in one way — to stay out of mine. It's not the best partnership, but I love the man like a father, and I can't very well tell him to get his shit together, now can I?

Also, getting out of the car on a stake-out to go on a food run is not part of the protocol, but thankfully, for the time of year it is, it's easy for me to blend right in with all of the other people.

December in Chicago is a crazy time. I guess

December in any city is pretty crazy, but in Chicago, it's another world. It makes it easier to blend in. There are lights all around, snow on the ground, people enjoying the festivities. Oh, and let's not forget about ice skating in Millennium Park — the people can't get enough of that. So, considering people tell me that the way I walk, dress, act, and I guess my overall demeanor screams 'cop' from a mile away, it's a good thing I can just blend in with the other people walking around, as I walk back to the car with a big bag of food. I make sure to hide my badge behind the food, as well. It's not uncommon for a detective to be walking down the street. Still, considering this is a residential street, I don't want to give our suspect any reason to get suspicious today, all because Walter had a craving.

Before I left Walter to get his food, I begged him to keep an eye on our suspect's apartment building to make sure we didn't lose him. As I walk back to the car, I can see through the back window that Walter is playing with the sun-visor instead of doing his job. Sometimes I don't know what to do with this man.

I open the driver side door and interrupt Walter's playtime, "Cut it out. I left you here to watch for the suspect, not to play with yourself!"

"Finally! I'm starving," Walter replies.

I hand him a sandwich, and he wastes no time diving in. With food in his mouth, he asks, "Hey, you didn't forget my backup sub, did you? You know I like to snack when these things run late."

What did I tell you...

"No, Walter, I did not forget your backup sub. And how many times do I have to tell you, a sub is not a snack, you fat ass."

Walter rubs his stomach. "It is to me."

We both laugh it off — that's just Walter.

I could tell at times the fat jokes bother him when it isn't just the two of us. He's not a fan of the other detectives making fun of him. He once was a great detective, now he's the butt of every joke — it can find a way to get to the best of us. However, when it's just him and me, he knows I don't mean anything by it, I only say it for his own good. I worry about his health.

After both of us chowing down for a bit, I know its's time to get down to business. We had been here for a few hours before my little run, and now we need to go over these case files again. It's only a matter of time before our suspect comes out of his apartment.

"Alright, so let's run down these case files one more time."

Walter threw his sub on the dashboard and pulls out a large file with the cases we've been working on.

"Well, our girl, Jenna Meyers, went missing the same way as all the others. It was reported by a friend of hers about thirty-six hours after she first went missing. Luckily, the friend was the one that mentioned we should look into this suspect — Steven

James. I guess he was Jenna's boyfriend. Apparently, he has been acting strange ever since she went missing."

I take a second to reprocess all this information. "I think if my girlfriend went missing, I would be acting strange too."

"Yea, well, something doesn't seem right about this guy." Walter says, with a bit of unease in his voice.

"What do you mean?" I ask with a bit of confusion at Walter's actual detective work.

Walter flips to a different page in the file. "I had one of the guys at the precinct dig into our suspect."

That makes more sense...

Walter continues. "He looks like all of our missing victims."

"How so?" I ask, immediately forgetting my original bias in Steven's favor.

Walter explains, "Outside of his name and address, this guy is basically a ghost. There is no family, school, or job history. Hell, he doesn't even have a social media account. I'm not saying that makes him our kidnapper, but something doesn't feel right."

Okay, now I'm a bit more interested. Walter could have led with that before we came on this stake-out. "Alright, does that mean he's our next victim or is he picking off people with his off-the-grid patterns?"

"Eh... couldn't tell ya." Walter's interest in the case has reached its limit, and he grabs his sub.

God damn... Walter's attention span is getting smaller by the day.

"Walter, we need to figure something out here. Just because of all that doesn't mean we're any closer to solving this." I ponder for a moment. "But, I'm pretty sure something is up with this guy."

Walter takes a few more bites, and a curious gaze comes over him. I honestly thought, for a moment, he was thinking of the case — for a moment. Then he speaks.

"Maybe we should just head back to the station and re-evaluate the situation with these missing pasts. I feel like we're missing a piece of the puzzle. Even better, we can do it over a drink!"

That's all he wants, to wash down his sub with a bourbon. Oh, if I didn't mention it before, the only thing Walter enjoys more than food is booze. I swear he used to be a great detective, one of the best, in fact. However, a long time ago, all of that changed — a case that actually changed both of our lives. I was only a kid, and he was a young detective. But that's not important right now. I just didn't want you to get the wrong impression of him; he really does mean well — most of the time.

After brushing off his idiotic comment about

grabbing a drink while on a stake-out as we wait for our only lead in over a year on a high-profile case, I calm myself and respond.

"Not yet, you lazy ass..." Okay, so maybe I wasn't completely calm. "I still want to talk to this guy. He has got to know something."

Walter is not happy with my decision. You see, he is technically the lead detective. He has seniority over me which makes him in charge of these cases. However, that doesn't mean he isn't on thin ice at the precinct. It's my work that keeps him employed, so he still does what I tell him to.

"Fine... I still don't get why we can't knock on the guy's door," Walter says, upset that his plan to skip out on work has failed.

"Come on, Walter, you know how I like to do things. If we hang out here, we might get a better idea of who this guy is. Have I ever steered you wrong? No... I haven't."

"You got a point. But I'm going to finish my sub." Walter looks down at the rest of the sub on his lap. "Come here, you beautiful angel."

I can't help but laugh as the next words fall from my mouth. "My God, you really are a fat bastard! Maybe you should have listened to my aunt all those years ago when she told you to lay off the fatty foods. Who knows, maybe you would still be in the shape you were in back then."

"Whoa, whoa, whoa! Don't let this body fool you.

I can still kick your ass up and down this block... I just don't want to." Walter shoves the rest of the sub in his mouth.

We both crack up. Walter chokes a bit on the last bite of his sub, which only makes us laugh even harder.

I slap his arm, as I see movement coming from Steven's apartment.

Steven lives in a duplex apartment building, so I can see him exit directly from his place and walk down the stairs to the street. We're parked just a bit down the block, so we aren't spotted.

I see Steven walk in our direction.

"There he is," I tell Walter.

"Finally," Walter says.

THE CHASE_
JOHN

WALTER AND I EXIT THE CAR AND BEGIN WALKING toward Steven. Thankfully, with all the people still out on the street coming home from last-minute Christmas shopping, we blend right in. Well, sort of. Walter has his cheap suit on, which makes him stick out more than I do — and I have a badge hanging around my neck. So, we try to play it cool, but a 30-year-old and a 60-year-old with no gifts, 3 days before Christmas, both screaming 'cop' doesn't help much. It's only a matter of time before... Yup, we've been made.

Steven stops dead in his tracks. Walter and I look at each other. Should we run toward him? He isn't running. What should we do? Wait, why is he looking at me like that? It's like he knows me. It's kind of freaking me out.

We both take a step forward, and he turns and runs. Here we go.

We chase after him. He's fast. Shit, he's really fast. We're doing all we can to keep up, and I'm doing all I can to make sure Walter doesn't have a heart attack while we chase him down.

Clearly, Steven knows something; otherwise why would he have taken off like this?

Walter screams out, "Chicago Police! Freeze!"

It doesn't faze Steven in the slightest — he keeps going. I didn't think that would work. He clearly knows we were police, and Walter just wasted his breath.

Steven turns down another side street, hoping to lose us, but we stay on him. We're far behind, there is no way we can keep up. This guy must have been a track star — wherever he went to school. I'll have to ask him if I ever catch him.

I have an idea. So, I yell to Walter, "Stay on him!" Then I turn down an alley and double back.

I know there is only one way to catch up to this guy. Usually, I would just say it's time to cut our losses and we'll find him another way, but after a year of searching with only one lead, I can't let this one go. So, I sprint as fast as I can with the little energy I have left — God, I can only imagine how Walter is feeling right now — and I make it to the car. I have to track them down. Thankfully, I track Walter's phone because I tend to lose him in the slew of bars or fast-food joints throughout the city more often than I'd care to admit.

Once I find which way they're heading, I speed off in their direction.

Now, I know my boss won't be happy about this one, mainly because we don't know what this guy knows, but I feel that this guy has something to do with these missing people. Also, if you could have only seen how he looked at me, you would know I need to do something extreme. It was like when he saw my face, he knew it was over for him. I need to find him.

So, I speed toward Walter and Steven. It seems that they ran down an alley — I just hope Walter is close enough behind that he didn't lose track of Steven.

I fly down the wrong way on a one-way street. I pull into a driveway and slam on the brakes in front of Steven. I thought that this would slow him down or, at the very least, make him jump onto the hood of the car as if he were attempting to jump over it but fail. However, I don't know what the hell I saw. Maybe it was the impact that affected my vision — yea, the impact, which yet another strange occurrence from tonight.

As Steven was running toward me, and Walter seemed to be miles behind him, I could have sworn his eyes began to... to glow red.

No. That's crazy. I'm going to just chalk that all

up to the shitty food that Walter makes me eat. It's messing with my head.

Either way, he hit my car, and that's what the impact was. Steven charges at the car with such a force that it was as if a bus had hit the front end. I actually thought to myself, 'I'm glad I had my seatbelt on.' It shakes me up a bit and it knocks Steven out cold, which gives Walter enough time to catch up, pin him down, and cuff him. I have to say, for a skinny guy, he is strong as hell.

By this point, I was back to my usual self. I get out of the car and shake off any crazy ideas I have about mentioning this to anyone. As a detective, you never want to say you saw something strange in the field, especially someone with glowing red eyes. They'll put you on desk duty for that, and who's going to protect Walter if I'm riding a desk?

Walter looks up at the dent in the car with shock. He glances back down at Steven, who was still on the ground but not fully conscious, and said, "God damn! How fast were you going!?"

As Steven is now slowly waking up, concern washes over him. He looks at Walter and blurts out, "You have no idea what you're getting involved in. I'm not who you think I am, and trust me when I tell you, none of this is what you think it is."

Walter laughs him off and helps him up. Then, he hands Steven off to me.

I say, as I toss him in the back seat of the car. "Okay, well, why don't you tell us all about it on the way to the precinct? We have a few other questions for you anyway."

I slam the door on Steven, and through the window of the back door, he gives me the same look he did when I first saw him. It was almost as if he was staring into my soul — and I'm not enjoying it at all. I don't know if he's our kidnapper, but those eyes are telling me he's guilty of something. Is that wrong for a detective to say? I know, I shouldn't prejudge a person. So, let's just keep that between us... Deal?

I walk over to Walter — he's looking at the damage to the car.

"How the hell are we going to explain this to the guys at the motor pool?"

"I guess we just tell them some doped up suspect charged at it," I question my own answer.

"You think he's on something?" Walter asks curiously.

"I don't know," I sigh. "Can you explain how he not only ran as fast as he did but also was able to crash into me like that?"

"Yea, I guess you're right. Are you okay, by the way?" Walter put his hand on my shoulder. "You look like shit. Maybe you have a concussion."

"Yea, I'm fine." I want to say something about Steven's eyes to Walter. I mean, it's just Walter; I know I can trust him, but I also know he'll worry. "Let's just get this guy back to the station."

"Whatever you say, boss," Walter says without argument.

PERP WALK_
JOHN

On the way to the precinct, Walter spends the entire time fighting to catch his breath. Honestly, I was considering calling him an ambo just for the oxygen tank. The guy is breathing like a bulldog. I know Walter will be alright; he tends to breathe like that even when he hasn't been chasing down a suspect.

I guess the strangest part of the car ride is Steven. I can't shake this feeling that he thinks he knows me somehow. He won't say a word. He just keeps watching me through the rear-view mirror. I noticed it in the beginning, and I looked back at him. I mean, why not, right? But it's so odd making eye contact with someone through a mirror. I'm not sure why, but it's not the same as looking at someone directly. So, I stopped. After I stopped looking back, I could just...

well, I could just feel him staring at me. I guess that's what criminals do. They want to get into the mind of the person that arrested them. It only furthers my assumption that he knows something I don't. I will get to the bottom of it, though.

We finally arrive at the precinct: Fourth floor — Homicide and Missing Persons Unit. Steven seems very dodgy. He isn't trying to run, he just seems to be looking for someone. Maybe an associate — who knows...

Ben Tyler, a detective and a close friend of mine, is sitting at his desk in the bullpen. I give him a nod when we walk in. He knows how long Walter and I have been working on this case without a solid lead, so he knows how vital this suspect is to us.

While keeping a tight grip on Steven's arm and guiding him through the bullpen, I turn to Walter and say, "I'll drop him in interrogation."

"Got it. I'll be at the desk," Walter replies.

I head to the interrogation room and leave Steven cuffed to the table. He isn't looking at me like he was in the car. He seems terrified now. Maybe the walls are closing in on him. Criminals who know they have no way to answer the questions about to be hurled at them often get that look. His look seems a bit deeper than that, though.

I leave the interrogation room and head back to our desks. The bullpen is set up, as I can imagine many large city police departments are, with a checkered pattern of white and slighter darker white linoleum tiles with gray walls. Rows of metal desks two by two facing one another. It makes for the perfect echo as your footsteps click on the tiles.

Walter is sitting at his desk with his feet up. Great. Every time he does that, he pushes his garbage onto my desk. Walter's sits directly across from me, which is not the best workspace for me, as he leaves me open to an infestation of ants at least once a month. Why you ask? Well, the constant empty food wrappers or dribbles of pop left in the can at the bottom of his garbage - which I beg him to wash out before tossing — tend to attract bugs. We have a janitorial service, but they clean the main garbage in the bullpen, not the small desk garbage, which we aren't meant to put food into, anyway. Walter doesn't like to follow instructions.

All of this drives me crazy. I like things to be clean. My desk, as you can guess, is orderly. However, I will admit, it borders on the obsessive. I may or may not pull out the ruler from time to time to check the spacing between my keyboard and monitor, monitor to my mouse pad, mouse pad to pencil holder, and my pencil holder to my file folders. I wouldn't say I have O.C.D. or anything, I just spent years around Walter, so cleaning up after his messes has caused me to create a bit of a pattern. It makes it easy for the other detectives to play pranks on me, though. Hilarious pranks.

Walter looks like he is trying to fall asleep. I knock his feet off the desk. "I'm going to get some of this paperwork out of the way before we question him. Another thing, we really need to dive into these strange backgrounds more before we go back in there. I feel like we're missing something."

Walter leans forward in his chair, but then his phone rings. I *almost* had his attention. His phone is on his desk, and I notice that the caller ID reads "unknown caller." Walter almost let it go to voicemail but gives his phone a double-take, like he recognizes the phone number — strange.

He picks up his phone, gets up from his desk, and responds to me before walking away. "Yea, yea, I'm with you. I just gotta take this first..." He starts walking down the hallway near our desks, and I could only hear him for a second before he was out of earshot.

"Yea, hello?" Walter says.

Maybe he was expecting that call. Who knows?

Oh well, I try not to get too involved with Walter's business. Besides, I have work to do.

I'm looking over these files, and none of this makes any sense. These cases mean something — each one of them with the exact same profile, just like Steven James. Each victim has a first and last name, they have an address, but they have no past. How in the hell, especially in today's world with everyone connected to something, can you be a ghost? I don't get it. Steven knows something. He must. I'm looking at these files, and it's like they just appeared one day. How do they pay their bills? Don't their friends ask questions? Friends! Jenna's friend — Walter mentioned that Jenna's friend was the one who reported her missing, but he didn't say a name. Where are the notes of that?

I flip through all of our files, but there is no contact information. Not even a name. Who filed this report anyway? Probably Walter — I really need to stop giving that guy responsibilities...

Speaking of Walter, here he comes now. "Hey, Walter, what was the name of the friend for our girl?"

He looks out of it. He walks over to my desk and just stands, almost in a trance. The sound of my voice somewhat snaps him out of it. He looks at me, his eyes glazed over, and almost with a whisper he speaks. "What? Oh — I don't know."

"Shit, Walter, what the hell happened to you?" I sat up in my chair with concern.

Walter was more, I guess you can say, awake now. "No, nothing. It's just been a long night." He wasn't making eye contact before, but he is now. Staring right at me, he says, "Hey, I got a great idea."

"You want your other sub, don't you?" Honestly, he looks sick — I shouldn't make jokes, but it was just too easy.

Walter stares a hole through me and calmly says, "No... Asshole." I knew I shouldn't have made jokes.

He follows that up by saying, "It's just been a long night, and it's already late enough. Cain's Pub will be open for at least another two more hours. How about I finish up the paperwork, and you get a head start over there? Just have a bourbon and wait for me."

I sit back in my chair — something is wrong here. "Are you sure you're alright? You never offer to finish the paperwork."

"Yea, I'm fine. I just want to get the hell out of here. It's been a long day; you know I could use a drink. Not to mention, it'll take you at least two hours to do the damn work."

"Well, that's because I do it right!" I respond with a laugh.

Walter shrugs me off.

I think about it for a second. I mean, I could use a drink too. "Okay, well, what about Steven?"

"We can let him sleep in a cell for a few hours, and we can question him in the morning," Walter says with a bit of excitement, as he is sure he convinced me to cut the night short. "Besides, you know we will be better off once we've had some rest. And we can track down the friend in the morning too."

Okay, he's got me. I'm exhausted, and I could use a drink too. "Fine — I guess you're right." I can see the excitement on Walter's face. "I'll get Steven over to booking while you finish this up. But we have to get back here early tomorrow. You know we can't hold him long without charging him."

"No," Walter is quick to respond, "Don't worry, I'll take him over when I'm done here."

That was strange.

"What happened on that call?"

Walter's eyes widen. "What do you mean?"

"Well, for the first time, you're offering to take over all the work." I laugh. "All I'm saying is, whoever kicked your ass on that call, be sure to thank them for me."

"Oh…" Walter chuckles. "Yea, like I said, I just want to be able to get out of here at a decent time tonight — and we both know that won't happen with you doing the work, you God damn perfectionist. So, why don't you just meet me at Cain's, so I know you're not looking over my shoulder. Just know that the first round is on you tonight!"

"Yea, yea, I got it! I'll have a bourbon waiting for you!" I grab what I need and head for the elevator.

Waiting for the elevator door to close, I take one last look at Walter. I swear something doesn't feel right, but he said he was just tired. He wasn't one to keep things from me. Walter and I are always honest with each other, so I rarely question him. Keep in mind that since I was 17 years old, it was just the two of us. I didn't have a father growing up, my mother and my aunt were gone. We never hid anything from each other. I figure if he wants to tell me what was on his mind, he will. More than likely, it would have been at Cain's after a few too many drinks. Until then, I know he's alright because if he hasn't told me yet, it isn't that important.

The elevator door finally shuts, and I'm off.

A PICTURESQUE LANDSCAPE, JUST LIKE something straight from a fairytale. Rolling hills, tall trees, and autumn leaves falling almost daily. This is The Garden. It's a magical place to live, and the people here have always enjoyed every moment of it — until today.

Near the center of the village, on some of those fallen leaves, are trickles of blood. It isn't until the village square that the carnage is at its peak.

Giants lay bloodied and broken and scattered across the fields with no sign of life. Yet, women are kneeling next to each of them — crying out for them. If only they could be woken.

Throughout the devastation, more blood is being spilled. Not giants or human blood — Angels.

Raphael, an Archangel, is standing tall with his wings stretched wide. They are feathered like a bird, white in color, but with a beautiful golden glow. He is standing over Azazel.

Azazel, just a standard Angel, has lost the glow to his wings, as they lay slumped over his shoulders while he kneels on the ground. Azazel has specks of blood splattered across his wings from the fight. He is defeated.

Raphael holds a battle sword and is hesitant to strike... but ready. He would prefer other actions.

Men from the village rush to the side of the women who are still weeping near the giants; this may be the only time to get them to safety.

Azazel looks up at Raphael, and with a sigh, he pleads, "Brother... Please..."

———

Unknown Valley, After the Flood

A woman walks through a narrow, unknown valley along a riverbed.

She wears a pristine white tunic with a red shawl that covers much of her face, and fiery red hair peaks out through the shawl. One would question why she would be wandering in such a strange and possibly dangerous place.

She approaches a crater filled in by rocks and

boulders near the river. The woman raises one arm — on the palm of her hand is a strange symbol that seems to be a cross between a brand and a tattoo. Then, she stretches her shoulders and out extends two blood-red, leather-like wings that closely resemble those of a bat. However, these are enormous in stature. The thin skin of her wings are nearly translucent as the sun beats down on them.

With her arm still raised, she gently flicks her wrist at the crater and telekinetically removes each rock and boulder.

From under the rubble, a face appears — Azazel's face.

WALTER'S JOURNEY_

JOHN LEAVES WALTER AT THE PRECINCT TO handle the paperwork and book Steven for the night. He heads out to Cain's to get an early start on the Whiskey bottle that usually has Walter's name on it. However, tonight, that bottle will be calling John's name instead.

As the elevator doors finally close on John, Walter's demeanor, which had noticeably changed after his mysterious phone call, dropped even more. He no longer pretends to be 'just exhausted' as he put it for John's benefit. Something was clearly on his mind.

He glances at the paperwork left behind on John's desk. He places his hand on a file that he was meant to be working on, then holds in thought. After a brief moment, he brushes it aside and takes off toward the interrogation room where Steven is being held.

Steven sits inside the interrogation room, still cuffed to the table, legs bouncing up and down with nerves firing away. Walter walks into the room and removes the cuffs from the table.

"Get up," Walter says calmly.

Steven is confused. "What?"

Walter grips Steven's arm and forcefully stands him up. "I said, get up." He snaps and cuffs Steven's hands in front of his body, then ushers him out of the interrogation room.

While walking through the bullpen, Ben notices Walter with Steven. Walter's work ethic, well, to put it politely, is... lazy, at best. Ben knows that Walter is unlikely to do anything at all. So, for him to see Walter booking a suspect is rare; but not only that, Walter's face is making it seem as if there should be some reason for alarm here. However, Ben knows better than to get in Walter's way, so he leaves him be.

Walter and Steven take the elevator from the 4th floor to the 1st — Booking.

They approach the Desk Sergeant, who is deeply invested in his crossword puzzle. "We booking him for tonight?"

Walter quietly responds, "No, orders came down — they want him out of here. I gotta take him to Cook County."

The Desk Sergeant is confused. It's not typical protocol for a detective to transfer someone to county lock-up. Let alone in the middle of the night. More importantly, when that certain someone is only a suspect.

"You do?" The Desk Sergeant asks with great curiosity.

"Yea, I don't know, man." Walter is trying to play it cool. "I was just told to get him out of here. That's all I know."

The Desk Sergeant wants to call this one in, as he knows something doesn't seem right, but his crossword is calling out to him. "Yea, okay. Just sign here." He hands Walter a clipboard.

Walter signs and they head for the parking lot.

In the parking lot, Walter stays silent but with a firm grip kept on Steven's arm.

Steven looks at Walter. "Listen, I know you're just doing your job, which is why I'm not trying to run again. I'm a good guy — I'm on your side. I know it doesn't look like it, but we all want the same thing." Steven is working hard to convince Walter to listen to him. "You and your partner seem like good guys. Well, your partner does at least — no offense — you're just a bit rough around the edges. So, trust me when I say, this is just not the kind of bullshit you want to get caught up in."

They take a few more steps, and Walter seems to ignore every word that Steven said. Steven gets upset and snarls, "Goddammit, are you even listening to me?"

Walter quickly and calmly responds, "No. Shut up."

Steven is not happy.

They get to Walter's car and he shoves Steven in the back seat. Steven's hands are still cuffed in front of his body as Walter is about to shut the door. However, Steven notices something strange. Steven sticks his foot out to keep the door from closing. With fear in his voice, he speaks, "My God... Your eyes..."

Walter's eyes, typically blue in color, have been slowly transforming. Ever since they made it outside, something has taken control and caused the transformation to be complete. There is no longer blue in Walter's eyes. The color has been replaced by a swirling red cloud forming around the pupil. It's almost hypnotic. Steven is terrified.

In a calm voice, Walter responds with, "I don't know what you mean." Walter attempts to shut the door on Steven once again, but Steven pushes back.

"You spoke to him — didn't you?" Steven says with a slight tremble in his voice.

The swirl in Walter's eyes begins to spin a bit quicker. "I don't know what the hell you're talking about." Walter brushes Steven off.

"Okay, well, I said I wasn't going to run, but I think that's my cue." Steven immediately tries to force the door open. He attempts to stand up from the back seat, but Walter forces him back down with ease. Steven tries to fight back with all of his strength, but it appears that, somehow, Walter is stronger than ever.

When Steven wasn't able to fight back against Walter, a realization washed over him. Steven became more frightened than he already was. Walter grips tight on the chains between the cuffs and utters a spell in Latin. "LIGATUS MANUS."

The cuffs on Steven's wrists begin to glow for just a moment. Suddenly, the glow fades, and Steven's fear made much more sense. He understood how Walter, the same man who nearly passed out on the car ride back to the precinct just because he ran a few blocks chasing him down earlier in the night, now was so much stronger. Steven understood why his eyes were now cloudy and red, instead of the blue they once were. He understood why Walter had been so quiet, and to be honest, acting a bit strange. Steven understood all of this because there was something different about Walter.

Steven looks at Walter with fear in his eyes and tries to speak, but nothing comes out. It was as if the breath was pulled from his lungs all within an instant. Then, he tries once more, and with a tremble in his voice, he is finally able to get out what he knew was the one thing he wished he would never have to say again, "Azazel."

Steven hoped to never speak that name again,

and when it left his lips, it was as if a piece of him died because he knew he was no longer talking to Walter.

Walter, who had been monotone and stone-faced most of the night, had now relaxed, as if hearing the name Azazel had somehow snapped something inside of him and allowed him to relax. That's because Walter had checked out for the night — well, ever since his mysterious unknown caller back at the precinct, that is.

"Ah, Stevie, Stevie, Stevie. I've missed you, buddy! Where the hell have you been? Oh! You see what I did there? Never mind that, we'll have plenty of time for jokes soon enough."

Azazel, the same Angel who was defeated in The Garden, the same Angel who was buried alive in the unknown valley, is here in Chicago. Over the years he has become a bit more twisted. He uses crude humor as his scare tactic.

"You see, my new pal Walt here has plans to take you to see me. I won't be sticking around for the drive, though. No — this guy has so much heartburn, I can't take it anymore. So, I'll just see you soon."

Azazel used his phone call to infiltrate Walter's mind and is now possessing him and taking him for a ride. Most of the night, Walter was set on a sort of cruise control. He was given a set of tasks — get Steven to Azazel and get John the fuck out of the way — but Azazel had the power to take over if need be.

Azazel points to Steven's spelled cuffs, "Oh and don't go running off on me now. These little babies might as well have been made from Hellfire Forged Steel — and you know how much that shit kills! You try to pick that lock in any way, and my good buddy Wally will be picking pieces of you out of his car until Judgment Day. You understand? Good! Okay, see you soon!"

As soon as Azazel stops speaking, he, or should I say Walter, immediately returns to the monotone and stone-faced drab he was throughout the night. He shuts the back door on Steven, who is now too terrified to even plot his escape.

Walter slowly walks to the driver's side door, enters the car, and drives away.

FALLEN_

FALLEN NIGHTCLUB — WHERE THE BEST OF THE
worst come out to play in Chicago. This is Azazel's
place; he loves to live extravagantly. It's... well, you'll
see once they go inside.

Walter pulls up to Fallen and parks right in front.
Steven is still in the backseat, too afraid to escape.
Walter exits the car, walks around to Steven's side,
and pulls him from the car. Walter is gripping
Steven's arm and walking him to the front door of the
club.

Steven decides the only thing to do is plead for
his freedom. "Listen to me — you have no idea who
this guy is or what you are walking into. You have to
let me go. At the very least, call your partner.
Dammit — you need to listen to me!"

Just like before, Walter ignores Steven.

They approach the doorman of the club, and

calmly but with confidence, Walter asks, "Where is he?"

The doorman responds, "Follow me."

He leads them through the club. Steven is still cuffed, and Walter is still gripping his arm tight enough to leave a handprint on him.

At a quick glance, it looks like any nightclub with loud music, drinking, and dancing; but as you look closer, you can see why Fallen stands out among the rest.

Everyone inside seems to be completely entranced by the environment around them. There is the main stage at the far end of the bar with a DJ booth. On both sides of the DJ are two smaller stages with half-naked male and female dancers. Scattered around the club are other smaller stages with half-naked dancers as well. However, the stages aren't the only places people seem to be taking their clothes off. The place is... sinful.

They are led into a VIP lounge in the back of the club. As they enter, they immediately cross paths with two colossal security guards. The guards do not make a sound, nor move a muscle — they don't even look at Walter or Steven as they come through the door.

The lounge is dimly lit and it has that 'seedy backroom' vibe that makes you want to shower as soon as you leave. There is artwork hanging on the walls depicting battles of Heaven and Hell — Hell is winning.

The music in this room is different — it's softer and menacing. Several topless women are dancing up against each other in the room. They all appear to be in a trance. Two women are dancing on a man at the end of the room who is sitting in a throne-like chair.

The man — Azazel.

He is no longer the Angel he once was. He has Fallen from Grace. His wings are hidden under his over-priced tailored suit. To the women in the room, he is just a man. Steven, however, knows better.

Why he would need to place these women in some form of a trance to dance with him is the question. Azazel is a handsome man. Most importantly, since they believe he is just a man, there is no reason to fear him. He's average height, well built, black hair, and a devilish looking goatee that suits him quite nicely.

The doorman stops Walter and Steven in the middle of the room. He grabs two chairs, places them behind both men, and forcefully sits them down.

Azazel leans forward in his chair and speaks to the doorman, "Okay, you can go now. Take the girls with you. They shouldn't be here for this."

The doorman rounds up the women that were dancing but leaves the guards behind. The dancers fall in line and don't seem to mind being herded out of the room like sheep. The trance they are under is almost identical to the trance Walter was under.

Azazel looks to Walter with a curious gaze and decides to wake him — just a quick snap of his fingers and he's back to his old self again.

Walter snaps back to reality and looks around. He mumbles under his breath, "What the hell is going on..."

That's when Steven jumps in, "I told you not to get involved. Walter, meet Azazel."

Walter notices Azazel and immediately jumps to aggression, "Who the fu—"

Azazel cuts him off by placing one finger over his own mouth, making the 'shh' gesture. Walter immediately goes quiet. However, this time, Walter was not in a trance. This time, Walter was fully awake, just unable to speak. He is terrified and frozen from fear in his chair.

"I'll be with you in a bit," Azazel says to Walter before turning to Steven. "Now, I'm going to remove your cuffs, but I don't want you running off on me."

Azazel takes one hand and flicks his pointer and middle finger together in the direction of Steven's cuffs, and they vanish.

Steven rubs his wrists where the cuffs once were and nods toward the security guards. "Why not? Are you going to have those big bastards back there beat me to death if I do?"

"Oh, those guys aren't real," Azazel says calmly.

"What?" Steven asks, confused.

Azazel begins cracking himself up. "Yea! I thought it would have been hilarious to have a couple of big oafs guarding the door. You know, since I can pretty much do whatever I want! They're just a mirage!"

Azazel is still laughing hysterically. Then, to prove his point, while still laughing, he waves his hand toward the two guards, and they both vanish.

Steven hesitates for a moment. "That's really strange."

Azazel's laughter stops abruptly. "You're no fun."

Steven knows why he is here, and it isn't to laugh it up with an old friend he screwed over. Steven takes a breath, "Listen, I—"

Azazel interrupts Steven with a loud shout. "Enough! We both know why you're here."

He places his head in his hands and tries to calm his nerves. Steven and Azazel were friends at one point. Long ago. Steven turns his back on him. Azazel is trying to remember a better time.

Azazel finally stands up from his throne and begins to pace in circles around Steven and Walter.

"Ah... Steven, I don't understand. I mean, I was a friend to you. I took you under my wing. No pun intended. You're a demon, Steven."

That's right, Steven is a demon. A pure Hellfire forged demon.

Azazel continues on, "I know that you weren't a

fan at first, but none of you Tormented demons are. I just figured that by now, you would have stopped rebelling against Hell and joined up with The Born or The Mundane demons."

There are different forms of demons; each has their own unique gifts, their own strengths and weaknesses. However, we won't get to that just yet, but soon enough.

"Azazel, listen—" Steven interjects.

"No, no, you listen." Azazel cuts back in. "I want to forgive you, I really do. But you stole from me. Truthfully, I would have been able to forgive that." Azazel begins to get more upset. "However, what I cannot forgive — no, what I will not forgive — is who you've been working with."

Azazel stops pacing right in front of Steven and looks him in the eyes.

Steven tries to remain calm, but the fear takes over him. With a trembling voice he speaks, "I... I don't know who you're talking about."

Azazel doesn't respond. Instead, he backhands Steven in the face. The force from the slap causes the front two legs of the chair Steven is sitting on to lift off the ground. The chair begins to tip over. Azazel uses his Angelic abilities to telekinetically catch Steven and the chair and sit him upright. Steven now has a gash on his cheek from the slap.

"It's that bitch!" Azazel snaps. "Beth... She has been chapping my ass ever since the 1800s. But this time, we've come too far for you, her, and your little dream team to mess it up. So, first things first, where did you hide the Obols you stole?" Azazel then grabs the back of Walter's neck. "Oh, and if you say you don't have them, I will take Walter's head and shove it up your ass."

Azazel enjoys threatening people, and he tops this one off with a crooked smile. Unlike others who make odd threats, Azazel will actually follow through, and Steven knows that.

Steven was quick to give up the answer. "They're on a boat!"

"Boat? What boat?" Azazel let go of Walter and then brushes imaginary lint off his shirt as if it were all in good fun.

Steven, who is still feeling Azazel's hand against his cheek, is cringing while spitting the words out. "There's a boat docked in the Ogden Slip. I wanted it to be near the Hellgate just in case I needed to get back. There is a spell casted on it so mortals can't see it."

Azazel paces around the room in thought. "Did Beth cast the spell?"

"No, I swear!" Steven quickly responds. "I don't even know where she is."

"Oh, Steven, you were doing so well." Azazel grips Walter's neck. "You know, I consider myself a nice guy. So, I'll let you decide how deep you would like Walter's head to go."

"Please, just let me explain!" Steven yelps. "Beth runs the faction against Hell, yes, but I haven't seen her in years. She has been doing everything from the shadows. I just get messages sent to me. I was given a message on where to find the boat, and the details about it. Rumor has it, her powers are stronger now than ever before, and she has another witch helping her. So, she doesn't need to be out in the open anymore."

Azazel slowly walks back to his throne and sits down. "How much stronger?"

Steven, who feels that he might have bought himself more time, relaxes a bit. "I'm not sure. You know that she was always a strong witch, even before she became a demon. After she became one of the Tormented, she was given even more power; we all know that. And I've heard that she has teamed up with someone that can challenge anyone — even you."

Azazel is not happy to hear that. He enjoys being the most powerful being on Earth. It's what sets him out among the rest. As you know from all this talk of Beth, Steven is not the only demon on Earth. Because of that, you can probably imagine, Azazel is not the only Angel either. However, Angels are the most powerful out of the bunch, and out of them, Azazel reigns supreme.

Azazel stares down Steven with fire in his eyes,

and with a calm but stern voice, says, "No one can challenge me."

"What about the boss?" Steven says, hoping to knock Azazel down a peg and thinking this might give him a chance to escape if Azazel is fazed by the comment. "She was the one to give your wings back to you, wasn't she?"

Steven was wrong. Azazel wasn't thrown off by that comment, only angered. Azazel quickly stands up from his throne, rushes at lightning-fast speed over to Steven, grips his shirt, pushes against him, and tilts his chair backward. Holding him in a suspended state, Azazel screams in Steven's face. However, it's more than a scream. It's such a deep bellow that even Walter begins to tear up from fear.

"ENOUGH! Down there, she may be in charge, but on the surface, all of you answer to me. No matter what our plans are — understand?"

Azazel sets Steven back down on the ground and begins to pace around the room again. He becomes eerily calm and stops moving right in front of Steven. "You know, I think I'm about done."

"No! Wait—" Steven begs.

"Yea, I think it's definitely time for a little reconditioning," Azazel smirks with the thought of Steven's punishment. "Let's face it, you're either telling the truth and you don't know where she is or you just won't crack — either way, you're useless."

Steven begins to breathe heavily at the thought of reconditioning. "No! Azazel, please! You don't have to send me back down there. You're right, we were friends, and I ruined that, but I can make up for it. Let me go back in, and I'll find out more information for you."

Azazel begins to feel pity for Steven. He walks closer to Steven and places his hand on Steven's shoulder. "Oh, buddy..." Then Azazel winks. "No."

Azazel removes his hand from Steven's shoulder, and red clouds began to swirl in his eyes — exactly like they were in Walter's. However, it was different this time. For Walter, it was subtle. Steven only noticed it because he has seen them before, and he knew what to look for. With Azazel, once they began to form, there was no way to ignore them. They just have a way of drawing you in.

The clouds are just the beginning, as they eventually light up like flames until he reaches his ultimate power. Finally, his wings burst from his back. The magic of it is enticing — his wings burst without shredding his suit in any way. Azazel appreciates order and cleanliness and wouldn't tolerate wearing anything dirty or torn.

His wings are no longer as they were before Falling from Grace. Once pearl white and pure from Heaven, now feathered with a pale-red tint. There is a strange symbol branded on the inside of the left wing. It looks like something from an ancient language — like something you would find carved on the inside of an Egyptian pyramid.

With his wings stretched wide, Azazel peers into Steven's eyes and says his goodbyes to an old friend, "I promise this is for your own good. Do me a favor, though. Say hi to the boss for me when you get home."

"No! Please!" Steven yells in fear.

Azazel raises one hand in the air as his wings appear to flex. The room begins to glow, and nothing else can be seen but the light all around. When the glow fades, only Azazel and Walter remain.

Azazel looks to Walter and is startled. "Oh shit! I forgot you were still here. Well, I guess I don't need you anymore."

Azazel's wings are still stretched wide, and Walter is frantically trying to get a word out but is still stuck by Azazel's trick from earlier.

"Yea, I know, Fallen Angel got your tongue; it happens to the best of us. Listen, I'm doing you a favor here — I felt that heartburn of yours, and no one should be living through that."

Walter thrashes his body against the chair. So, Azazel decides to show just a bit of empathy.

"Oh, fine... but don't say I never did anything for you." In a mocking tone, Azazel continues, "Any last words?"

Then, Azazel annoyingly waves his hand toward Walter allowing him to speak again.

"Wait!" Walter shouts immediately. "I can be of use to you. I'm a cop, and I know a lot that goes on in this city. You said you're looking for someone, and I can help you find her."

Azazel pauses for a moment in thought.

"If I have been looking for her since 1871, then what makes you think you can find her now?"

Walter feels to have Azazel right where he wants him. "I'm very resourceful. I only want one thing in return."

Azazel paces slowly. He takes a step toward Walter, "Hmm... Eh..."

Azazel flexes his wings one last time, raises his hand toward Walter, and the room lights up.

A LONELY DRINK_
JOHN

Cain's Pub — the best cop bar in the city. Okay, so maybe it's the only cop bar in the city, but who's counting?

Walter and I come here after a particularly tough shift, which is why I'm sitting here tonight waiting for him. I'm surprised I'm the one waiting for him. To be honest, it's usually the other way around. I'm the one who is usually finishing up the paperwork while he is here knocking back round after round.

I don't mind though; the bar is great. It's a traditional Irish pub. Wood lines every inch of the place, from the tabletops to the bar, and dead center of the bar is a giant brass bar-tap. I don't really need anything from the tap because I'm more of a bourbon guy myself. I can thank Walter for that. He made sure I kept a taste for it the second I turned twenty-one. Between you and me, it was more like the second I turned eighteen, but again, who's counting? Also, there is a small stage in the corner of the bar. The owner, Neala Cain, will occasionally bring in live music. Tonight is a local band and they don't sound half bad.

The band just finished a song and they decide to take a quick five-minute break. That's when I check my phone and realize how long I've been sitting here waiting. It's been almost a full hour, and still no Walter. I haven't even received a call or text from him yet either. That's not like him. I should check in with him, just to make sure he isn't screwing anything up.

I call, but it goes straight to voicemail. All I hear is, "Hello, you've reached Detective Walter Finch. Please leave me a message."

That's not like him to have his phone off.

"Hey Walter, I'm here at Cain's. You must be really having a hard time with that paperwork..." I laugh, but the truth is, I'm slightly concerned. "I know you were exhausted tonight, so I'm thinking you finished up, went home, and forgot to call. I'm going to finish my drink and call it a night if you're not here soon. So, hurry your ass up!"

I hang up and swig my drink. I'm sure Walter isn't coming. I'm also sure he just went home for the night, so I might as well just call it quits.

I flag down Neala, she's also the main bartender here.

As I mentioned, this is a great place to come and

relax after a long night, but Neala is the main reason we all come here.

At only 5'2", she would take on any of the cops in here, even after taking down a few pints and a shot or two. Also, most of the guys go crazy after her. I can't help but admit that she's gorgeous with her reddish-blonde hair that matches her fiery attitude, but I wouldn't dream of flirting with her. For starters, we're just friends, and I know that, and I am damn glad to call her a friend. Also, she would definitely beat the shit out of me if I got out of line, and I'm not ashamed to admit that either. I mean, there's a reason she owns a cop bar...

"Hey, Neala, can you close me out, please?"

Neala walks over and pulls a small server ticket book from her back pocket. She rips a page out and puts it down in front of me. I already have my money in hand and lay down what's needed to pay my bill.

Neala points to the now watered-down drink next to me that was meant for Walter. "Where's the old man? You know I love it when that flirt walks through my door."

I shake my head. "Who the hell knows? He was supposed to finish up a couple of things at the station and head right over. But, like you said, he's an old man. Maybe he got tired and went home instead."

We both laugh, but my laughter quickly halts as I become concerned all over again.

"I'm just surprised he didn't call. It's not like him."

Neala takes notice and tries to cheer me up. "Well, it looks like drinks are on him next time."

"Yea, you try telling him that." We both laugh again.

I slam what's left of my drink and stand up from the bar.

"Alright, well, I'm done for the night. I'll see you later, Neala."

I grab my phone off the bar and turn to walk out.

"Have a good night, John," Neala said. "Oh, and make sure you tell Walter that you weren't the only one he stood up tonight!"

"Will do!" I wave as I walk away.

I head for the door and decide to call Walter one last time as I'm walking out just to be safe.

The phone, again, goes straight to voicemail.

"Hello, you've reached Detective Walter Finch. Please leave me a message."

He must be asleep. I hope.

"Hey Walter, I'm calling it a night." I really hope he's sleeping... "I'm hoping you're just at home. It's not like you to pass up a free drink, so do me a favor and call me when you get this. Oh, and Neala was sad to have missed you, too. I'm starting to think you may have a shot with her after all." I laugh, hoping to end the voicemail on a good note.

As I'm about to hang up the phone I decide to say one last thing.

"So, I'll see you in the morning."

A NEW DAY_
JOHN

PRESENT DAY
Gideon Detective Services, Chicago

It has been nearly two years since Walter was last seen. In that time, so much has changed. I fear that I am coming unhinged. I spend most of my days locked in my office — no, not the small desk space I shared with Walter on the 4th floor of the Chicago Police Precinct. It's now my own Private Investigation office.

I am no longer a detective with the Chicago Police Department. My law-and-order days have been reduced to catching people cheating on their spouses. This allows me to fund my own personal investigation into Walter's whereabouts. I know he's out there somewhere. Unlike the people that we were investigating together, he has a past. He has a family — me. People miss him. I don't care what anyone else says, he was not a dirty cop; he did not let Steven James escape that night.

There's a knock at my door. It's more than likely another crap case. I used to care about the well-being of people — I wanted to help. Why can't people just help themselves?

"Come in," I yell.

The door opens. Thank God, it's not a case... It's Ben Tyler. He still works for the department. He and I came up in the academy together, and we've maintained our friendship throughout my transition. He's the only person who has remained on Walter's side through all of this. At least he says he does. I know he wants to tell me to give up, but he's my friend, and he knows what Walter means to me. So, he comes to my office every few days to make sure I'm still alive. He's a good friend.

Ben grew up on the South Side of Chicago. He became a cop to try to fix things from the inside — we all know how rough the Chicago Police Department can be. He also understands what it's like to grow up without a father, as his was brutally taken from him. However, his story is much worse to live with than mine will ever be. I was always grateful I never had to witness such brutality like he did. But that's not my story to tell.

THE TOMB / 53

That's one of the reasons we became such close friends. I guess trauma can bring people closer. We became brothers. Neither of us had siblings of our own, so we became each other's family, and we've stuck to it. Whenever we were in need, we were always there for each other. Over the last two years, he's made sure to stick by my side no matter how hard I've made it for him. I guess I should really begin thinking of a way out of this funk I've been in. I am thankful he hasn't tried to push.

Ben takes a seat in front of my desk and places a bag of food in front of me. He looks around the office — I can't lie, it *is* kind of a mess. The once orderly John Gideon is gone; I even have a beard now. It's small, mainly stubble, I kind of like it though. Wait, where was I? Oh, yes...

Ben was scanning the room. "Damn, John, you need to get a maid."

"Come on, Ben, this place is perfect!" I technically wasn't lying. At one point in time, it was perfect. That was when I unpacked the first box...

"Yea, sure..." Ben shakes his head. "I'm serious, though. When is the last time you left this office?"

"I have a lot of work to do." I ignore the question.

Ben doesn't like that I'm ignoring him. "That's not an answer—"

"Listen..." I get a bit upset. "Walter has been missing for nearly two years, and if the roles were reversed, he would be doing everything he could to find me."

I knew immediately I was wrong for getting upset. I don't apologize, though. I just hang my head in shame for acting that way toward my one and only friend. Ben understands that I didn't mean it.

"I know that, and I know he was like family to you. So, I understand why this is so important." He hesitates to continue speaking. "But... it might be time to accept that he didn't disappear."

Okay, now I'm a little pissed. "What are you saying, Ben?"

Ben sighs. "Come on, John, you know what some people think happened that night — he was dirty, and he let your guy go."

I want to defend Walter, but I know how long Ben has been holding onto this, fighting to not say a word. So, I bite my tongue and let him speak.

"Now, I've tried to stay on Walter's side throughout this entire time — but I saw him leave with your suspect that night. I thought he was taking him to booking, but something didn't seem right about it. I knew better than to get in Walter's way..." Ben stutters a bit as he tries to get this next bit out. "But... but now I think maybe it was my fault. Maybe I should have stopped him."

I sigh. "It wasn't your fault Ben, and Walter wouldn't do that. I know things haven't been perfect for him on the force for a while, but he was a good cop. I just need to find the answers." I dive right back into my files.

Ben really wants to get through to me. I know that. I guess I just don't want to hear it. I must have become a bit thickheaded from all those years spent around Walter. God knows you couldn't get anything through to that guy.

He tries another approach. "I hope you do. You know I always liked Walter. He's your family, and you're like a brother to me, so I want to do whatever I can to help you. But don't you think it would have been easier if you were still with the department?"

I never actually told him why I left — the real reason. Ben wants to fix the department from the inside; he wants to rise to the top and make real changes. If I told him what the real issues were, I'd be worried that it would force his hand and make him step back. So, when I left, I just told him it was too hard to be there without Walter. I think it might be time to come clean, though.

"Ben, I never told you the truth as to why I left." I try not to get upset thinking of it all. "The truth is, the Chief of Police himself wanted me to close the missing person case on Walter after only six months of searching. Chief Armers told me I was to either close the case or hand in my badge. So, I gave him my badge." I hesitate to finish my thought, but he needs to know. "It would make a lot less sense, if... if he hadn't done it before."

Ben doesn't seem to comprehend a word of what I just said, which is understandable; I was a bit cryptic. Instead, he looks at me, confused, and simply asks, "What do you mean by that?"

I need to collect my thoughts for a moment. This isn't something I've thought about in years, and a story I've never had to tell.

"Well, you already know that when I was a kid, my mom disappeared, and I had to live with my aunt."

Ben knows all of this, which only makes him wonder where all of this is going.

"Yea, but what does that have to do with this case?" Ben asks.

"Well, Walter was assigned to my mom's case. That's actually how I met him." I pause for just a moment. "I didn't have a father; you know that too. So, I guess when Walter came around, he took pity on me at first. He eventually became someone I truly looked up to. He was a better person back then. He's the reason I wanted to become a detective."

Ben looks even more perplexed now than before. "John, where is all of this going?"

"When I graduated from the academy, he told me something that had been weighing on him. At the time, I just thought he was getting something off his chest. At that point, he had let himself go and had begun hitting the bottle a bit more often, so I always took what he said with a grain of salt.

However, now I'm starting to think it meant something."

"What did he say?" Ben sits back in his chair — pretending to care about a story he already knows. I tend to babble on about things before I get to my point.

I hate to admit it, but since Walter has gone missing, I've slowly progressed into a madman. I've spent my days rereading every file I have over and over. So, to Ben, this most likely sounds like the ramblings of someone who has lost it. I'm surprised but glad he hasn't written me off yet.

"Obviously, he never found my mom, but the reason isn't because of bad police work. His captain told him he had a choice — either close the case or hand in his badge. Sound familiar?"

Ben is in shock. "Wait, wasn't his captain—"

"Yea..." I cut him off. "Chief Armers. At the time, his captain was Armers."

Ben's jaw nearly hit the floor. "Why the hell would he get involved in both cases?"

That's a great question...

"I have no idea, but if I can get to the bottom of Walter's case, I might get some answers on what happened to my mother too."

Ben is in complete shock. "This still doesn't explain what Walter was doing with Steven that night. But if it gets you answers, I'll do whatever I can to help, you know that."

"I know. Thank you," I say, thankful for Ben's offer and for his understanding.

I glance down at some of my files. Unfortunately, they aren't exactly the ones I need to really get to work on this case. Which is why it's been so long and still no luck.

"The problem is, I've been racking my brain thinking what could have happened that night. Walter's attitude changed so drastically. I felt that there was something wrong, but he just kept telling me he was tired." I begin to get upset with myself. "Goddammit, I should have pushed harder."

Ben pulls me back from the edge. "No, John, it isn't your fault. I saw him that night too. I could tell something wasn't right either, but I didn't stop him. That's how Walter was; every day was a different attitude. He was just a grumpy old man, and no one liked to get in his way."

Ben's right. I loved... no I can't talk like that, he's still out there — he is still alive... I *love* Walter like my own father. He has his ups and downs, but I can't give up on him too. I've spent too much time on this to just throw in the towel now.

"I just feel like if I can restart everything, I can finally get some answers. The only problem is, without access to the last case we were working on, I'm screwed."

"What would you need from me?" Ben asks, knowing that's what I'd hope he would do.

"Well, if you're offering..." Ben shakes his head after my comment, and I continue on. "Would there be any way you can look into the last case Walter and I worked on? Also, anything I had on Walter from the last six months on the job? Armers made sure I didn't take anything important with me when I left. All I have now are the older case files that I was able to sneak off with."

"Yea, I can try. I'm actually heading into the precinct now. I'll call you when I know more."

I knew I could count on Ben. If there is one thing I know, it's when I have a problem, which I seem to have a lot of lately, Ben will be there for me.

"Thanks, Ben."

"Yea, anytime. Just do me a favor, please?" he says with genuine concern in his voice.

"Of course."

"Clean yourself up!" He laughs. "I mean, look at you, you have a damn beard!"

We both chuckles.

"What?! I like it!"

THE CALL_
JOHN

As I have no open cases, other than Walter's, of course, I decide to work from home the rest of the night.

Home for me is a tiny one-bedroom apartment in the city. It's actually not that bad — it's only a few blocks away from my office, which means I can walk it, and... okay, so I lied, it's not that nice. It's about as nice as my office: small, unorganized, full of old files, and a lot less furniture than an adult should own. But it works for me.

I'm going over some of the information I have on the old cases I was able to sneak out of the precinct before I left. Most of it is garbage, and I know it doesn't have any valuable intel on there for me to use, but it doesn't hurt to look at anything I can.

The only thing that peels my eyes from the page

is the sound of my phone ringing. Ben is calling... Did he find something?

"Hey, Ben."

On the other end of the phone, I can hear him slightly whispering as if he did something wrong.

"I think I might have found something."

Holy shit. Ben found something. Wait, I tell myself, it's been almost two years, and that was really fast, and I can't get my hopes up just yet.

"What do you got?" I say as if I don't really care. Even though I do care — I care a lot.

"I think I found the guy you and Walter were after that night. Steven."

Okay, now I care a whole hell of a lot. I nearly jump out of my chair. Fuck, I might have even pissed myself a little — but that stays between you and me. Deal?

"Wait — I thought he went missing along with Walter..."

"Yea, that's what we all thought, but as I was going over some of these files, I got a hit on an open case from just a few months ago," Ben says, still whispering, but this time a bit softer.

"So, what are you saying? Is he in the city?" I'm even more excited.

"I think so. But listen, I don't think I should be talking here anymore... Shit..." Ben freaks out.

"What happened?!" I start to get nervous.

"As we speak, files are being removed from the

system. Someone doesn't want us looking at these. I was able to print some of this stuff out, thankfully, but the rest is gone. John, we need to meet now."

Ben is terrified. I've never seen or heard this side of Ben before. I need you to understand, Ben is basically more muscle than man. He grew up in a tough neighborhood, where he was forced to be even tougher on the outside in order to get by. So, believe me when I say, there is not much that scares him. I think diving into a potential conspiracy is making him a bit on edge, and that's my fault.

"That's okay. You did more than enough. You need to get out of there. You know that diner by my place — Darcy's?"

"Yea, I know the place. I'm leaving now — I'll see you in twenty," Ben says, then hangs up the phone.

THE FOLLOWER_

JOHN EXITS HIS APARTMENT COMPLEX AFTER HIS phone call with Ben. He is cautiously optimistic that the information Ben has will lead to something. Let's face it, after all this time searching with no leads, John has become more of a realist than an optimist. In today's society, that's a better trait to have anyway.

Right outside his front door, there is a newsstand. It is later in the evening, so there aren't many people there at this time of night. However, one should stand out, but John doesn't notice her.

She is only pretending to read a newspaper. She seems to be watching John, but his focus is still on the call he just had with Ben; he has his blinders on.

It's dark outside, so it's hard to make out much more than just a silhouette. She's a short, petite woman, and alone at night at a newsstand "reading" a newspaper; this should stand out to a former homicide detective that has become increasingly paranoid.

How long has she been watching him? No. I guess the real question and the most crucial question — why is she watching him?

THE PICTURE_
JOHN

Ben said he would be at the diner in twenty minutes. The wait is killing me. What information does he have? Is this what I needed all along? Why the hell didn't I ask him sooner?

I guess when I look at the bigger picture, I just didn't want to get Ben caught up in all of this. I know that Armers has something to do with all of this — he has to. Why else would he be involved in both my mom's case and Walter's? I just didn't want to risk Ben's career because I can't let something go. I just knew in my heart that now was the right time to ask for help. Ben was ready to throw in the towel on Walter... who knows, maybe even on me. I couldn't have that.

Ben is my best friend — he's my brother. Damn... he is actually the only family I still have left, and I've been doing a shitty job showing him that. All that, while he has done a damn good job being there for me. Even though I haven't made it easy. I guess that's what family is about. I promise, once this is over, I'll be a better brother to him. But right now, I need to find Walter.

I only live a couple blocks away from the diner, so I wait the full twenty minutes to leave my apartment — which feels like twenty years. I hit the street, pass the newsstand, and say 'hey' to Pete who owns it. He's a good guy. He never charges me for my morning paper. Plus, I got him out of a few parking tickets while I was still on the force, and Ben helps him now. That guy has the 'worst luck' when it comes to parking meters, or so he says. He's a good guy, just trying to get by. A bit nosy, though.

I finally make it to Darcy's Diner. The couple blocks felt like forever. Ben is already at a table waiting for me. He seems to be on edge while gripping his coffee cup.

Ben doesn't wait for me to get comfortable to begin speaking. "I'm pretty sure Armers is onto me. Now, considering he knows you and I are friends, I'd say he's onto you too."

A server comes to our table, and I order a cup of coffee. Then, I think about what Ben had said about the files being removed from his computer. "Well, he did have someone erase the files. So, I'd say he might be onto you."

"Smartass..." Ben shakes his head at my comment.

THE TOMB / 67

"Another thing — in all your time on the force, how often did Armers pay us a visit in the bullpen?"

My eyes widen. "Wait, he talked to you?"

"No, he was with the captain. I got out of there before he had a chance to." Ben pauses for a moment. He seems to be rethinking his anxiety. "I don't know, maybe I'm just paranoid, but when I was leaving, Armers looked directly at me and waved. I mean, I have never said a word to the man in my life." Ben starts to get a bit excited. "So, I'm a little on edge now that he's starting to notice me. Especially after I was looking into your case files that he himself had previously shut down. Not to mention, they just vanished from my computer as I'm going through them."

Okay, maybe he has a reason to be a bit paranoid.

"Well, I would say that he was just trying to be friendly with the wave, but I doubt it. Dirty cop or not, he was always kind of an asshole."

The server returns to the table with my coffee. I take a sip before I continue on.

"Listen, Ben, you looked into something that he clearly didn't want you to. I would just watch your back for a little while."

As I say that, I think to myself, what the hell did I just get Ben into? Ben is a great detective, and he has plans for his career. He doesn't just want to ride out the same position until his pension. He is on the fast-track to a promotion. He should be a Sergeant by this time next year, and I may have just thrown that all away for him.

I think back to all the stories Walter told me. Before he took on my mother's case, he was a rising star on the force. He had one of the best records for a homicide detective and was close to his Sergeant's badge as well. His goal was to make it to Chief someday. He never made it beyond detective. He was a detective for just over twenty years and couldn't break through to another level. All because of one case. One case that changed both of our lives forever. I don't want to do that to Ben. That's why we need to get to the bottom of this. I've already pulled him in too far. If we can't figure out what the connection is to Armers, then Ben might as well cancel his gym membership and start chugging bourbon — because he'll become the next Walter Finch.

As my mind is racing and Ben's legs are bouncing around from anxiety, I notice a woman walk into the diner. I know, probably not the best time to lose focus, but she is the most hypnotic woman I have ever laid eyes on. Is she looking at me? Should I say hi? No... I haven't even gotten to the good part of Ben's information yet — but I just can't seem to take my eyes off of her.

She's sitting alone, and she orders a cup of coffee. I'm not usually like this. I'm a gentleman — I swear. I don't know what's wrong with me. I feel like she has some kind of hold on me. I can't quite figure out what it is that's drawing me in. Is it her smile as the server walks to her table? Her medium-blonde hair? Her hazel eyes with a small tint of gold under these diner lights? Which, I must say, until tonight, gave me a headache, and now I can't get enough of them. Or is it the way that she knows I can't stop looking, but she is so confident that she just doesn't seem to care? She continues reading her paper, the same one I read every morning. Honestly, I mainly get it for the crossword... oh, she flipped the page, and I see she is just about to start the crossword. She's perfect.

Oh, shit, Ben's mouth is moving. Is he talking or chewing? No, we only have coffee... he's talking.

"Wait, I'm sorry — what did you say?" I interrupt him.

He notices my eyes are elsewhere but is a bit too upset with everything to bother looking back. He repeats everything I just missed.

"I said — that's easy for you to say — you don't have to go back to the station any time soon. So, how do you expect me to lay low?"

Oh, right... that's what we were talking about. I nod along like I was listening the entire time. Ben sees right through me and shakes his head — we've been friends far too long; he knows me too well.

"Ben, if this case leads us to where I think it will, then Armers will have either been involved in the kidnappings or at least covered up for them all along. I don't have a badge anymore; there is only so much that I can do. If you end up being the detective that can solve this thing, think about what this will do for you!"

Okay, I'm not proud of it, I really am not, but I might have been playing to his ego a bit on this one. I just need him to relax because I would never let anything bad happen to him like it did to Walter. I have lost too many people in my life, and I will *not* lose another. No matter what it takes. I just really need his help getting to the bottom of this, for Walter and for my mom.

Ben takes a long, slow sip of his coffee — he has a flair for the dramatic — and then gives me a devilish grin.

"Ah... Fine! I know you're just playing me, you dick, but fine. I might have to take some personal days to stay away from the station while we work on this, though."

I get so excited that he's willing to team up, that I slap my hands down on the table. I knew I made a bit too much noise, so I look around the diner to apologize to the people near us, and that's when I realize the woman of my dreams is gone. I pause for a moment, but then was right back to the joy that I would be working with Ben on this one.

"Alright, well, why don't you show me what you got?" I say to Ben.

Ben reaches for his briefcase and grabs a stack of file folders and opens one in particular.

"Like I said on the phone, we thought Steven went missing the night Walter did, but he must have just gone deep underground."

I lean into the table. "Why do you say that?"

Ben starts looking for a particular document while speaking. "Because I found something you're going to want to see. When I was pulling up some of the information, I remembered that, while you were still with the department, you put in for facial recognition through traffic cams on Steven and Walter. Luckily for us, no one ever pulled that request. So, I ran a scan of the cameras to see if we had a match. It turned out a few months ago, there was a similar case to the ones you and Walter were working on."

Ben finally finds the papers he was looking for. I couldn't believe what I was seeing.

"And apparently, a traffic cam was able to pick up Steven."

Ben slaps a picture of Steven down on the table, and it leaves me in shock. I honestly can't believe my eyes. This is the lead I have needed since day one. Just like back then, except this time, I am not going to let him slip away. However, at that moment, I realize something. If this picture was taken months ago, then where's Walter? Why wasn't Steven questioned? Ben would have seen Steven in the precinct, and he would have told me about this. My amazement turned to absolute confusion in a matter of seconds.

"This picture is amazing, Ben, but something tells me he isn't in custody."

Ben looks at the picture, upset with how he has to answer. "That's the weird part. It was just left in limbo. No one ever followed up on it."

"Armers..." I say with disgust.

Ben nods in agreement. "That's what I'm thinking. There is good news, though." He smiles. "The traffic cam that spotted him is only one block from the apartment you picked him up from that night."

My excitement comes flooding back, and I blurt out. "So, if he's still in the city..."

Ben finishes my sentence. "Then, he's at home waiting for you."

My face lights up. As this conversation goes on, we're getting closer and closer to the answers we need.

"Ben, this is unbelievable. This is the first solid lead — hell, this is the only lead we've had since Walter went missing."

Ben sits back in his chair, takes a sip of his coffee, and grins. "I'm happy to help. So, now what?"

Ben tends to get a bit cocky when it comes to his good work. He knows he is good at his job and even better at investigating cold cases than the average detective. As his close friend, I usually call him out for getting up on that high horse — but I'll let him have this one. He earned it. Plus, I know he isn't going to like what I'm about to say next.

"Well, now, I'm going to scope out the place."

He almost spits out his coffee. "Not alone, you're not! I'm not going to have you charging in there, half-cocked, and get yourself hurt; or worse!"

It seems Ben has very little faith in me. Half-cocked... I may have been a bit off my game lately, but I'm still the same man I always have been! He should know that by now.

"I won't approach him. I just want to know if he really is in town. If he is, then we will meet tomorrow and put a plan in place."

He just stares at me. "You know, this 'I'm the boss' shit may have worked with Walter, but not with me."

I chuckle. He was right — I always bossed Walter around. Not because I thought I was in charge or thought I was better than he was, it was just the only way we were able to get our job done. Walter loved having me as a partner because I got things done.

"Noted — and my apologies. It was just a habit with Walter, and I won't make it one with you. But I'll be fine tonight. If I spot him and need back up, I'll call you."

The truth is, I just don't want to get Ben involved any more than I already have. Ben prefers his work in black and white — a fine line between good and evil. He doesn't like things in shades of gray. However, where I'm going tonight will be in a deep shade of gray, and I want to make sure I have proof Steven is there before I bring Ben over that line even further.

Ben clearly wants to fight me, but he already knows what I've been thinking. "Fine. Just don't do anything stupid, okay?"

I smile. "I won't!"

FIGHT_
JOHN

I HAVEN'T BEEN BACK TO THIS STREET IN SINCE
that night. I haven't thought to check. Why would I?
I mean, this entire time, I've been working under the
assumption that Walter went missing because of
Steven. So, if that is the case, then why would he
come back to the place I know he would be? Unless
that isn't the case — either that or he is just an idiot...

It looks the same, minus the snow on the ground.
However, that does make it a bit difficult to blend in.
That, and it's just after midnight on a residential
street, and I'm just sitting in a parked car. Thankfully,
I'm not in what clearly looks to be an undercover cop
car this time. No, you see, last time was a 2018 Black
Ford Taurus. If that doesn't scream 'new and
improved unmarked cruiser,' I don't know what does.
I might as well have been in a Crown Vic with one of
those old school red bubble lights on the top.

This time I'm in my personal car — a 1992 Ford Bronco. It may stand out a bit, but not because people expect it to be someone tailing them. Yes, in my line of work, I have to follow people occasionally. Checking out cheating spouses leads me to follow people to hotels, bars or... some other undisclosed locations for undisclosed things, which is entirely the client's business and none of yours... See, now you got me off-topic.

What was I saying? Oh, yes! The Bronco... Plus, I've always liked this car. Not because of the white Bronco down the highway but because it's a cool truck! Besides, mine is black.

Back to the point!

I park just a few apartments down from Steven's duplex. I remember being here before, but my heart wasn't racing this fast last time. Perhaps it was because I had Walter here with me last time. It also could have been because the case wasn't personal. That's not to say I didn't care about the people I was searching for. I always cared about my cases; it's just this time it hits home. It's not only Walter, this could also be my mother.

I decide the best course of action is to just sit and wait. The same thing as last time. Steven will come to the window or leave his apartment eventually. I'll see him, I'll confirm he's in town, and then Ben and I will make a plan. It's 12:19 a.m. right now, so there's a good chance I'll be here a while, but I'm willing to stay all night if I have to.

———

Later that night

I feel like days have passed by, and no movement. I thought I could wait it out with patience but knowing that the only person with the answers I need could be in that apartment is killing me. I check my watch – it's only 3:37am.

I'm fighting myself to stay in the car, but my mind is racing. I tell myself that I can just peek through the window. The lights are on. Someone is home. If I'm careful, no one will know. This will confirm if it's him or not, and then I can just go home. No one will know — no one will get hurt.

I shouldn't, right? Ben would be pissed. Then again, Ben isn't here...

Screw this... I'm going.

I get out of the car, and the street is vacant. Before I walk across the street to head for Steven's apartment, I decide it's better to be safe than sorry. I may not be a detective anymore, but that doesn't mean I don't still carry a firearm.

I reach to my hip and remove a Sig Sauer P226 from my holster. I release the magazine to check the rounds, reinsert it, and then pull the slide back slightly to check the chambered round. I re-holster my pistol, and I'm ready. I hope I won't need this, but I remember him being strong enough to nearly total my car. So, if he's home and he spots me, I may need it.

I jog across the street and run to the side of Steven's duplex apartment. He lives on the first floor, which allows me to peek through the window without too much of a struggle.

I just look through the bottom corner of the window to be sure I'm not seen.

Holy shit...

It's Steven, and he's not alone. There's a man with him. He's a younger man, and they both are sitting around a coffee table, looking over what appears to be blueprints. Also on the table is a velvet drawstring pouch that Steven seems to be keeping a close eye on. He is twirling the string, and it's the closest thing to him on the table. It must be important.

Seeing Steven sitting there stirs up rage within me that I have not felt before. He was involved with whatever happened to Walter, I know it. Why isn't he in custody? I need to find out why.

I know I should call Ben, but I know he'll try to stop me from doing what I want to do. He'll try to arrest him, and I know Armers will just let him go. Why wouldn't he? He already let his facial recognition sit by the wayside. He let Walter's case go cold. I need to handle this my way.

I drop down below the window and think to myself — if I'm going to do anything, I need to be careful. The last time I chased down Steven, he was fast; I had to follow him with my car, and we know how that turned out. Now he has a friend who appears to be in better shape than Steven is, so I just need to be smart.

Or I can break in the back door... Yea, that sounds better. Ben is going to kill me.

I quietly walk to the back door and pick the lock. Then, I draw my weapon and enter the apartment. Thankfully, Steven and The Young Man that's with him are sitting at the front of the apartment in the living room, so I knew I was safe.

I enter the kitchen. The apartment is filthy, with grime on the walls, the cabinets, and the floor. There is no furniture in the kitchen, and I doubt in many of the other rooms. The only thing I could see through the window was what looked to be a few lawn chairs and a dirty coffee table.

I shut the door behind me as soft as I can and begin walking toward the hallway. As I start walking, I could hear Steven and The Young Man speaking.

"Everything needs to be in place tonight. Do you understand me?" Steven says. Judging by his tone, he doesn't seem to be too pleased.

I stop moving so I could listen better.

The Young Man speaks up, "I've already told you,

do not talk to me like that. I know the plan, now back off."

"Listen, I'm only in this mess because of you." Steven seems to be getting angry. "Azazel put me in charge, so just relax."

Who's Azazel? Is he their boss? Maybe he knows something about Walter, or maybe he had something to do with the kidnappings or whatever those blueprints are that they're looking at. I need to get a closer look at those blueprints.

I begin walking back down the hallway toward Steven and The Young Man in the living room. I'm not quite sure of my plan yet, but if I can just see those blueprints, then I can get out of here. Otherwise, I'll make... I don't know, a citizen's arrest, I guess.

As I get closer to the living room, with my gun still drawn, one of my footstep's creaks against the old hardwood floor.

I hear The Young Man speak up. "Wait... Shut up."

"Don't tell me to—" Steven is upset but is interrupted by The Young Man.

"No, shut up! I hear something."

Fuck.

"Well, why don't you go check it out?" Steven says.

I flatten my body against the wall.

The Young Man speaks up again. "You go check

it out! You're the one who is so happy to be in charge. Well, take charge!"

"Fine. Damn, you're lazy..." Steven gets up from the lawn chair and walks toward the hallway.

There is no way he is going to walk past me. I may be hidden from them for now, but once he gets in here, he'll see me. I need to do something.

Steven walks into the hallway and spots me. I panic.

My reaction is to attack. I draw on Steven, but he doesn't care. Instead, he lunges for my gun.

I do my best to keep hold of it, but he is as strong as he is fast. I throw Steven up against the wall, but he takes me with him. As he has my arm locked up, this knocks my gun from my hand, and it slides into the living room — as does our fight, and we land on the floor.

The Young Man stands up from his chair, and I fear he'll go for my gun, so I swat it to the other end of the room. However, he just stands there, laughing at us both. He doesn't seem to care that we're beating the shit out of each other.

The fight continues. Either I am out of shape or Steven is much stronger than anticipated because I am not winning this fight.

I'm doing my best to reach for my gun, hoping that having it back in my hand will calm things down again. That's when I realize The Young Man is bored with just watching. He still doesn't seem to care all that much; maybe he just wants this to end. He slowly begins to walk toward the other end of the room toward my gun.

I know that now is my last chance to take back control of this situation. Back... I never had it in the first place.

Steven has me pinned down and I'm using my arms to hold him back from choking me out. Finally, I catch a break. I throw his arms off to the side and throw a quick jab to his jaw, which doesn't seem to do much damage. I was expecting to hear him groan, instead I hear what seems to be laughter coming from him. However, it is still just enough for me to slip out from underneath him.

The Young Man takes note and moves a bit faster, so I dive the best I can from the position I am in to grab my gun. I reach it before he does.

I get to it first, lean against the wall, and take aim. My hope is that both he and Steven will stop moving, but The Young Man takes another step and reaches his arm out for me. Now, I'm exhausted, and I know there is nothing I can do to fight him off. He didn't join the fight between Steven and me at all, so if he wants to go a round or two with me, I will be a goner. Goddammit, I should have listened to Ben. Why the fuck don't I ever listen to Ben? If I get out of this alive, I swear I will listen to him more often.

As much as I don't want it to end this way, I know that there is only one thing I can do to save myself.

I steady my aim and fire three rounds point-blank into The Young Man's chest, and he rocks back from the impact — but that's all he does.

What the hell is going on here. He didn't drop. He... he didn't drop. Why didn't he hit the ground?

The Young Man looks at Steven, and they both start to laugh as if I had said something funny, as if I told them a God damn joke. I didn't, I shot the son of bitch. Didn't I? Did I get hit in the head too hard during that fight?

The Young Man looks at me and with a menacing tone says, "That kind of tickled. Do it again."

I'm still on the floor against the wall and I'm shaking. I don't know what to do. I must be dreaming. Because I now know for sure I shot him. There are three holes in his chest... wait, no there aren't. They just healed. What the hell is going on? There were three bullet holes. Now, there are just three holes in his shirt, with blood stains around it, but behind that is only skin.

I try to get words out, but I only stutter. "What... the..."

They both just look at me with a terrifying smile that keeps reminding me that something is definitely wrong. So, I ask, "Who are you people?"

Steven chimes in with a calming voice. "You know, in all fairness, I vaguely remember warning you to stay away from all this."

I'm confused. "All of what? What is this?" Now, I'm angry. "And where the hell is Walter?"

I won't drop my gun. Instead, I re-steady my aim. If it didn't work on The Young Man, I doubt it'll work on Steven, but it won't hurt to show I'm ready to use it again.

"Oh, don't worry about him right now," Steven answers and then points to my gun. "You can put that thing down. You're just going to end up hurting yourself."

Steven begins walking toward me, reaching for my gun. It's odd — he almost seems... well, I guess I would have to call it, polite. But I don't trust him.

"Back the fuck up!" I aim at Steven.

"Alright, alright, calm down." Steven chuckles when he responds. He takes one step back and continues, "What do you think you're going to do with that thing?"

I want to say something, I want to shoot, but I feel frozen. I still do not understand what's going on.

Steven smiles, "Exactly. You're not going to do anything. But hey, if it makes you feel better pointing that at me, then suit yourself."

The Young Man is essentially kicking his feet around with boredom. Boredom! Here I am, shitting my pants with fear, and he seems bored. Don't forget, it was no more than ten seconds ago that I shot him in the chest — but I guess I'm boring.

The Young Man turns to Steven and sighs. "Well,

I think it's time to go another route." Then, he looks at me. "You know, I didn't want it to come to this." He glances back to Steven. "Did I not say, I didn't want it to come to this."

"Yea, you did say that..." Steven responds.

The Young Man crouches down to look at me. "John, you should have just stayed away. It would have made things so much easier."

He said my name... Steven did not mention me by name, so how does this guy know me?

My voice trembles. "You know me?"

The Young Man stands back up. "Oh yea, we all know you, you're famous! Well, your family is. We all hear the tales of the famous Gideon family bloodline." Then he a playful chuckle takes over his voice. "I got shot by a Gideon! I can't wait to tell everyone in the pit! Look at me, I'm all giddy!"

I'm even more confused now than I was before. "What are you talking about?"

The Young Man throws his arms in the air. "Don't tell me you don't know your own history!"

"No..." I say, hoping for answers.

This entire time Steven had been looking confused and finally chimes in.

"Wow... I thought that was why you came for me that night. Now, I find out you're clueless!" Steven shakes his head.

Before I can ask what they are talking about, The

Young Man speaks up. "Oh well. Now you'll never know!"

Then things become a bit clearer. These aren't men at all. They are something beyond anything I could imagine — something I wouldn't even want to dream up. These men come from nightmares.

The Young Man extends his arm and, without touching me, I am lifted from the ground, and the air was pulled from my lungs in a single breath.

Steven looks to The Young Man, as he — what I could only say is — telekinetically holds me in the air and says, "Don't drag this out. We still have a lot to set up for tomorrow."

As my legs dangle nearly a foot from the ground and I gasp for breath, I raise my gun to fire, knowing this won't work but hoping it will at least break his focus. The Young Man uses his other hand and flicks his wrist in the direction of my gun, and it falls to the floor beneath me.

The Young Man begins to make a squeezing gesture with his hand, and now I feel pressure against my throat. Even though I know he's not actually touching me, I still claw at my neck out of reflex.

That's when I catch The Young Man's eyes... red swirling clouds that draw you in and light up brighter as he sucks the life out of you. I'm drawn in. I grow weaker and weaker.

He looks at me and says, "John, I want you to know, I am sorry I have to do this. You should have just stayed away. But lucky for me — at least I'm the one that gets to kill off the bloodline!"

Just then, a blast comes through the front door, which sends thousands of wood splinters scattering around the room hurling all around. Both Steven and The Young Man shield their eyes from the blast.

The Young Man shielding his eyes causes him to drop me, and the air rushes back into my lungs. I fight to catch my breath and try to focus to see who just saved my life.

Steven uncovers his face and looks to the hole in the wall where the door once was. He is in shock.

"Beth? Is that really you?" Steven is in awe.

Beth says... something... and gently swipes her hand toward Steven and The Young Man.

"IACTO."

This throws both of them across the room.

Steven and The Young Man hit the wall. The Young Man is out cold.

Steven tries to get up, but Beth goes in for one more attack.

"FRACTUM PEDEM."

She snaps one of Steven's legs.

"Ah! You bitch!" Steven shouts.

Beth reaches for the velvet drawstring pouch off of the coffee table that Steven was keeping close to him before.

Beth looks to Steven, "You should have stayed in Hell." Then, to me. "Come on, we need to go!"

I, for the first time, got a good look at her. This is the same woman from Darcy's Diner. Has she been following me? What the hell is she doing here? Should I trust her? Do I really have a choice? That's when I remember, there's something else on that table that needs to be looked over.

"Wait, the blueprints!"

Beth looks to the table, but she didn't want to risk it. Steven was already coming back for us. He had pressed down on his broken leg and reset the bone, and it begins to heal instantly.

"No time — come on!"

I'm still on the floor, so Beth grabs my arm, pulls me up off the floor, and takes me with her. We run through the hole in the wall where the front door once stood, and I think we're free.

Wait, is she slowing down? What is she doing?!

"Come on, I thought we have to go!" I yell.

Yup... she is definitely stopping. She's on the front porch, and I can't help but think this woman is crazy... beautiful. Goddammit, John, keep it in your pants! She's crazy — we need to go! But she stops anyway. She looks at the hole in the wall that she made her glorious entrance through and speaks whatever magic she speaks... oh my god, I really must have gotten hit hard...

With her hands raised to where the door should be, Beth speaks, "CASĂ ÎNCUIATĂ," and a flash appears across the hole for just a moment.

I'm at the bottom of the stairs stunned, as I still am not sure what the hell is going on!

Beth runs down the stairs and shouts, "Come on!"

I don't move. Mainly because I'm shocked, I'm terrified, and I'm not even sure if I'm really here. I'm pretty sure I made a terrible mistake by breaking into Steven's apartment tonight. I know for a fact that I broke into his apartment. I know for a fact I got into a fight with him. However, I'm almost positive he and his friend beat the shit out of me, and now I'm in a coma at Rush Hospital.

I stand there, watching The Young Man, who has regained consciousness, run to the hole in the wall and then be thrown violently back into the apartment as if he ran straight into a Linebacker from the Chicago Bears.

Beth realizes I'm not following her. She runs to my side, grabs my arm, yanks on it, and yells, "Get in the fucking car! That spell won't last forever!"

"Spell?" I say with utter confusion.

I sprint alongside her to my car, she gets in the passenger seat, and we take off. I can't stop checking my rear-view mirror and looking over my shoulder. Whatever she's talking about, she said it wouldn't last forever. Are they coming now? How long do we have? Who is she, who are they, what is all of this, and how do they know me...? My god, I have so many questions. She better have some answers.

I scream. "Ah!!!"

Beth just looks at me calmly. Why is she calm? It's freaking me out even more than I already am. "Who the hell are you? Who were they, and what is going on?"

"John, just breathe. I'm Beth, I'm here to help you."

She knows me too... Okay, so that guy was right — everyone does know me. I'm not a big fan of this newfound fame.

"Me? Why? I don't understand. Why do you all know who I am? And..." I'm beginning to stutter. "And what he could do... Who... Who were they?"

"I know none of this makes any sense, but we need to get somewhere safe, and I promise I'll explain as much as I can."

I can't stop looking over my shoulder. I'm driving erratically; I don't even think I'm on the right side of the road. But it's okay, right? I mean, this is all some fever or coma dream that I'm having from having the shit kicked out of me! I mean, why else would the woman from the diner be here? Unfortunately, the further I drive, the more I begin to believe it's real. The blood on my knuckles is drying, and my hands are sore from the fight; my adrenaline is pumping like I've never felt before — that could also be my mind playing tricks on me, but it just feels so real.

"John, I placed a spell on the apartment, so they can't follow us right now. They'll be out of there within an hour or so, but right now, we're safe. We shouldn't go back to your place though. I suppose your office is also out of the question. We can go to my place and lay low." She points. "Turn here."

"A spell?" I can't believe I'm hearing this again. She said it before we got in the car, and I don't think it registered then. Now that I know I'm not being chased, I'm hearing things properly. A spell... this is real life, not some magical world. What kind of an alternate reality did I stumble into?

"Just drive, and I'll explain when we get there," Beth says as she rests her head against the headrest.

How is she so calm? Is this her everyday life? I glance at her with a terrified gaze and drive on as she continues to point us in the right direction.

THE TRUTH_
BETH

As we pull up to my townhouse, John's heart is still beating through his chest. I know that because he won't stop telling me... I just hope after I explain what happened tonight, he doesn't have a heart attack.

We walk up to my house — from the outside, it looks like any townhouse you'd see in the city. A row of five homes lined together, all sharing a wall with the next, on a relatively quiet street for Chicago — you know the type. However, this one is a bit different.

We walk in the door and John's eyes widen. The townhouse is not just one unit. In fact, it's all five.

All but one door is spelled shut, so there is only one-way in. However, there is a second way out, but that is only for me to know. I built this place over the years to fit my recluse lifestyle — not to mention I have been hunted for the past nearly century and a half, so it helps to be secluded.

"This place is a mansion," John says with amazement.

"More like a fortress," I reply. "When you live the life that I do, you need a little extra privacy."

John continues looking around a bit, but I can tell he was too afraid to let me out of his sight. I didn't tell him to stay close, but he was still pretty shaken up from the events at Steven's apartment. I don't blame him; it can't be easy to be thrown around like a ragdoll by forces unknown.

I walk over to the bar and pour two drinks. I could see the wheels turning in John's mind from my last comment.

"And what kind of life is that?" He needs answers. Again, I don't blame him.

I walk over to him with drinks in hand. "It's hard to explain." I hand him a glass. He grabs his drink and gulps it down with ease. He points to the bar, and without saying a word, I know what he's asking for.

"Help yourself," I say.

He walks over and pours himself another. He's earned it.

As he walks back over toward me, I gesture for us to sit down on the couch. I place the velvet drawstring pouch that I took from Steven's apartment on the coffee table in front of us. It's a large sectional couch, which gives John plenty of room to sit as far from me as possible — and he does.

Once we sit, John says, "Beth, please, I need to know what's going on."

I know he is not going to like the answers I give, but he's right.

"Okay, I just need you to trust me." John does not look happy after hearing me say that. "Well, first of all, I'm a demon. And those two guys back there, they're demons, too."

John stares blankly for a moment. It seems that he almost laughs at one point, but then it appears he begins to think back on the night he just had.

After his brief pause, he calmly sets his drink down on the table. I'm not quite sure what he's planning, or what he may be thinking. Then, he quickly leaps up from the couch, reaches for his hip and tries to draw his gun.

I raise my hand and shout, "SUBSISTO," which is a small incantation in Latin to freeze him in place.

John is terrified. This is not something I wanted to do to him. He does not need this right now, and I need him to trust me.

With fear in his voice, he asks, "What are you doing to me?"

"I'm trying to show you, that even though I have this power, I am on your side, and I will not hurt you." I speak calmly to stress he does not need to fear me. "John, that bullet won't hurt me. If it makes you feel better, then shoot me, but I would prefer it if we just talk."

He seems to be calming down and he asks, "Can you let go of me?"

I nod 'yes' and lower my hand to release him.

John, thankfully, lowers his gun and sits back down.

"Thank you," I say. "Listen, I know this isn't easy, but it's only going to get crazier. So, I need you to just hear me out and trust that I'm on your side."

I swear, if looks could kill, this one would have done me in. John stares daggers at me, "You just told me you're a demon. How the fuck could it get crazier than that?"

I need to figure out where to start. Of course, I understand how all this sounds. I mean, if I were in his shoes, I would probably want to shoot me too. I'm glad he didn't. No, it wouldn't kill me, and yes, I would be able to heal, but that doesn't mean it wouldn't hurt. Have you ever been shot before? No — I didn't think so! And you're lucky!

"Okay, I'm assuming Steven and his friend were talking about a plan of some kind. I know how demons like Steven work. He tends to give up information when he thinks he's got everything under control. Idiots."

"Yea!" John says. "He said something about setting up for tomorrow. That's why I said to grab those blueprints. When I was in the room, I was able to see the building they were for, but not why they were looking at them. They were for the Water Tower Pumping Station downtown. I could see there was a second set of blueprints under it, though, that I couldn't make out." John grabbed the velvet pouch off the table. "All you wanted was this little bag, though."

"Shit..." I put my head in my hands. "I knew about the Water Tower blueprints, which is why I didn't grab them. I didn't know they had the second set, though. And this bag is much more important than you know. It's key to their plan."

John rustles it around and could feel what was inside. Then, he tosses the pouch back on the table.

"So, the key to their plan is a bag of quarters?" John said with confusion.

"No, one of the keys to their plan are actual keys, but they aren't quarters..." I open the pouch and pull out one of the coins to show John. "To anyone that doesn't know any better, it's just a bag of old coins, but these are no ordinary coins. They're called Obols, and it may be a small part — but it's a crucial part in their plan."

"Okay, well, what's their plan?" John asks without hesitation.

He wanted to shoot me just seconds ago, now he doesn't hesitate when I mention ancient coins. I'm not sure if he believes me or thinks I'm crazy and is just biding his time so he can run. I guess we'll see.

"Okay, well, demons have always blended in with

humanity and only a select few mortals have known. There are those like you, who stumbled onto it. Then, there are ones with gifts — witches. They fought against demons for centuries as they have tried to raise Hell to the surface."

"Do you mean like an apocalypse?" John chuckles. He thinks I'm joking.

"Yes," I say clearly.

John's demeanor drops.

"They have been trying to bring upon an apocalypse since the beginning. However, for the first time in quite a long time, they may actually succeed — and now I need your help to stop them."

"My help? You're — what? A super-powered demon?" John shouts. "I saw you break Steven's leg by speaking to it. Why would you need *my* help? Also, why would you even want to stop them? YOU'RE. A. DEMON."

Okay, so I understand where he's coming from, but that's a bit rude. I know he's frustrated, but I did just save his life.

"I'm not like the rest of them," I say, holding back my own frustration at his last comment. "There are different forms of demons and I definitely stand out from the rest. Like I said, witches have fought against Hell for centuries. When I was mortal, I was a witch. It's one of the reasons why I was able to regain my freedom back. But that's a story for another day, right now we have more pressing matters."

That probably didn't help John's trust level by me adding yet another layer of craziness to the mix — but I continue on anyway.

"Let me explain; there are two forms of magic — light and dark. As a mortal, I was tricked into practicing dark magic, which is why my soul was sent to Hell, and that's how I became a demon. The Being that deceived me is the same one that is now controlling everything here on Earth, and..." I really don't want to say the next part, but I know he needs to hear it. "And I think he is the same Being responsible for the disappearance of your friend Walter."

I knew this wouldn't be easy for John to hear, but I think he might be taking it harder than expected. He stands up from the couch and begins pacing around the room.

"Listen, I want to find Walter more than anything. I just still don't understand how I fit into this story."

I can tell this isn't going to get any easier...

"To understand that, you need to understand your past first." I sigh. "The last time Hell was this close to controlling Earth was back in 1871. When I met your Great-Great-Great-Grandfather."

"My what?"

John stops dead in his tracks. He sits back down on the couch. Except, this time, he sits just a bit closer to me. I think he is finally starting to believe me.

"He was a Lieutenant in the Chicago Police Department at the time. He, and a powerful friend of mine, helped me put Hell back in its place. Along with locking away something very dangerous that they are now trying to set free. Just like you, he stumbled onto something he didn't want to."

John is in complete shock. He doesn't know whether to believe me or not. I can see that in his face. I think he is just going with it because he doesn't know what else to do. From all he has seen tonight, what else can he do?

"So, that's why Steven's friend said my family is famous?"

I nod my head.

"Now, for their plan to work, they need to break open what's known as The Seven Seals."

John looks perplexed. "Wait, wait, wait... are you talking about the stuff from the bible?" He even laughs a little.

"Yea, but it's a little different than you think. The Seven Seals of Revelation were written as Hell's greatest trick played against humanity. The idea is it'll be horrible for a time, but the faithful will get paradise in the end. In reality, the only paradise is for the demons that are gifted with Earth for all eternity. And of course, the humans that they can torment while they are here."

"We need to tell people about this!" John begins to get worked up.

"Oh, yeah, great idea. Should we start shouting 'judgment day is coming?' I mean, I can make us signs."

I just wanted to make light of the situation, hoping to make him laugh. He needs a good laugh. Plus, it was nice to see him finally believe what I was saying. Unfortunately, he didn't like my joke...

"Sorry..." Maybe now wasn't the best time for a joke...

I just continue on. "The reason I need your help is that you're the only one who can access the armory with the weapons that can stop what's coming."

"How is that possible? I didn't even know anything about this." John questions.

"This armory is spelled to only open for someone within the Gideon Family Bloodline. You see, in 1871, a Hellgate opened, and Hellfire spewed throughout Chicago. It set fire to a large chunk of the city. Obviously, people don't know that it was a potential apocalypse."

John has a realization of what I am talking about immediately. "The Great Chicago Fire?"

"Yeah..." I say. "Unlucky for the city, but lucky for us. Because the only weapons that can stop what we're up against is steel forged in Hellfire. Once Hellfire scorches steel, it becomes charged with raw energy. Even if you re-forge it in any way, it won't lose its charge. And right now, there is a full armory waiting for you."

John is speechless.

"During the chaos of the fire is when I met your Great-Great-Great-Grandfather. After discovering the truth, he couldn't stand by and watch as these Beings rose to power. So, after we held off Hell, we gathered up as much of the steel from the rubble and stored it for times like these. After he was gone, I knew I needed to keep it safe."

John sits in silence for a moment. He needs to say something — I've been rambling on, and I'm afraid to say anything else out of fear that he'll run.

He looks at me and says, "You keep talking about something that is 'coming.' It makes me think it's worse than just Steven and his friend. So, what is it?"

"It's what the first Four Seals represent, and what we locked up in 1871. The Four Horsemen of the Apocalypse and their Champion: The Anti-Christ. We knew if we locked them away, Hell would not be able to break the final Three Seals. So, we sealed them in a tomb we built inside one of the abandoned tunnels under the Water Tower Pumping Station. The second set of blueprints you saw at Steven's were the prints to the abandoned tunnels leading them through the pumping station to the tomb of The Horsemen."

"What would happen if they were released?" John asks curiously.

"It would be devastation across the globe, but ground zero would be here in the city." For a moment, I was too afraid to let John in on how bad it would be but, once again, he needs to know the truth.

"After we locked them up, we thought we were safe, we thought everything was fine because we knew they could not get out. However, the spell was only strong enough for The Horsemen's physical bodies to stay in, but not their power. They were still able to influence the worst of humanity throughout the years.

"What do you mean?" John asks.

I held back for a moment, as I think back on all of this. I feel the heavy burden of the lives lost. I feel as if the blood is on my hands... I did not do enough to stop it.

"In 1918, the Spanish Flu tore through the world's population. It was a plague on humanity, and the spread could not be contained. I knew something seemed off, but I thought it couldn't be them... Then, in Germany, 1933, Hitler rose to power. Which led to the second World War, mass murder, a great divide in their country — and in the world. It was then that I realized that The Horsemen's power was being released through the tomb. In 1918, Pestilence came through, and in 1933, War came through. Each time, they grew strong enough to allow Death to absorb the lost souls. I knew if all four of their powers came through, eventually the Anti-Christ would be strong enough to break the tomb walls and release their physical form to allow Hell to break the remaining Three Seals and unleash Hell on Earth."

I say all of this with a heavy heart. John can't believe the things I'm saying — but there is still more.

"If they are released today, all of this would happen at one time. We would see a divide between people in our country as well as across the globe. There would be a plague sweeping nations that would be out of control. We would see war in our very streets by people who just want to fight for their own freedoms — their basic human rights. If famine is released, friends and neighbors would fight just for scraps of food or basic human essentials. And if The Anti-Christ is released, we will see a dictator in the making with untold power."

I'm choking back tears as I speak because I know that this could have been avoided. If only we were stronger — if only I was stronger. I could have stopped so much bloodshed.

"In 1918 and 1933 humanity was struggling. Because of that, awful people were giving The Horsemen the strength to power through the tomb walls. And you can see it again in today's society. When you look out in the streets, you see people protesting for equality — but they should never need to do such things. In today's society, people should be free. It's The Horsemen that keep them shackled, because there will always be the worst of humanity that rise to power on the backs of evil beings. Some knowingly, others unknowingly. Every time you turn on the news there is either a mass shooting or some form of bloodshed without reform — neither of which should be happening. Both events just add souls to the damned and fuel Hell's inevitable rise. We have people who are begging for equality and they are willing to risk everything for it, but evil keeps them down. As long as these Beings who fight to release The Horsemen stand among us, evil will always win the battles we face. And if the tomb opens and The Riders are released I can't even imagine what kind of carnage we will see. And my fear is that The Anti-Christ is growing stronger. We see world leaders allowing such chaos to grow stronger. Protests for freedoms are met with violent aggression instead of proper amendments to better our nation and the nations of the entire world. This is something I have seen in my long life before, and it did not end well. I understand this is a lot to drop on you, more than you were expecting, I'm sure, but I promised to answer as much as I could for you."

After hearing everything, John appears to be in shock, but thankfully he is listening and seems to believe me.

He picks up the pouch from the table. "So, I'm assuming these 'keys' open the tomb, then."

"No. Obols open Hellgates. There are gates to

Hell all over the world, but the main one is here in Chicago, near the Ogden Slip."

John rolls his eyes after my response. "Of course, it is..." As if to say, we don't already have enough problems here.

I continue, "These aren't the only ones. However, this will, at least, slow down their progress. You see, a Hellgate is the only safe way to and from Hell. And of course, us having these means there are fewer demons on Earth. The problem is — The Four Horsemen are not in Hell anymore."

"So?" John doesn't understand why that's a problem.

"So, unlike in 1871, there won't be a massive fire letting us know they are coming."

"Oh..." The realization of a potential disaster washes over John's face.

"Thankfully, the spell on the tomb will be difficult to break, but the Being in control will stop at nothing to get his way. There are more powerful demons in Hell that might be capable of breaking the spell, which is why I needed to steal these." I point to the pouch. "I need to stop them from freeing all Four Horsemen. However, they can still try to open the tomb and break just one seal at a time. The First Seal will release The Anti-Christ and Pestilence. If that happens, each seal will begin to break on their own as The Horsemen create more chaos in the world. This is why I need your help — I don't know if I can do this alone."

At this point, I'm all but begging John to help me. I know this is more than he has asked for and more than he wants on his plate, but this is bigger than him... and bigger than me — I need him.

He looks to the floor; I can sense that I might be losing him. Not that he doesn't believe what I'm saying, but it might be too much for him to handle.

"I don't know, Beth." He pauses. John sits back and thinks. "You know, when you said this conversation would get crazier, I didn't believe you. I guess I should have known better when you started it off by talking about spells..." John sighs. "Unfortunately, I think you're still holding something back, though. When you spoke about 'The Being' controlling everything, you didn't say human or demon. It's something worse, isn't it?"

He has me there... Too much of all this at once scares new demons, so I could only imagine how a mortal would react. When I learned the truth about the world, it was already too late for me. I just didn't want to scare him away.

"I was afraid to tell you everything."

"Beth, please..." He begs.

I sigh and reluctantly continue on. "Demons aren't the only thing outside of mortals that walk around out there. There are different forms of demons — a hierarchy, I guess you could call it.

However, the most powerful creatures on Earth are a collective of Fallen Angels known as The Watchers."

John stares blankly for a moment, then says, "Angels?"

I continue, "They immerse themselves in our everyday life and watch over humanity while doing Hell's bidding. Some of them have remained hidden from me, as they can do almost anything they want. They can even alter your perception of reality and make you see them or anyone else as someone completely different. Their leader, Azazel, likes to remain out in the open, though. He owns the Fallen nightclub downtown. I have spent years collecting information on them, and in doing so, I believe I found something useful for your investigations."

I hesitate for a moment, knowing what I am about to say will only fuel the rage within John. "I believe that's the last place Walter was before he disappeared."

I wait for John to speak. I want him to say something, anything. But it never comes. It was silent for what seems like an eternity as he stares at the floor. With all the information I have given him, he is just defeated, and understandably so. He cannot take anymore today.

"Listen, John, I know it's a lot. I won't lay any more on you right now. If this is something you can't be a part of, and you need to leave and focus only on Walter's case, I understand, but you can't leave tonight. Your apartment, your office — they all know where you live and work, and I need to protect you."

John finally looks back up at me, and with a quick response, he says, "So, you can get your weapons?"

Of course he would think that. "No. Because I'm a good person. Even if you don't believe me."

He smiles. Just a bit, but it was still a smile. This might have been the first time I've seen him smile since the diner. It's not a bad smile... too bad I've been depressing him all night. He might be starting to trust me.

I move in just a bit closer, "Stay here tonight." I try my hand at one more joke, "I think I may have an extra room for you."

He chuckles. It may have been a pity laugh for my bad judgment day joke early, but at least it was a laugh. I'll take it.

"Come on, I'll show you the way."

FAILURE_

Back at Fallen nightclub, Steven and The Young Man are unfortunately ready to admit to their failures.

Steven and The Young Man walk into the VIP Lounge and Azazel is sitting in his throne with two topless women standing on either side of him and another topless woman behind him rubbing his shoulders. He is not looking happy.

Steven tries to play off their blunder. "Hey, Azazel... How's your night going?"

Azazel is furious at Steven's attitude.

"How's it going?" He could hardly finish. Azazel scans around to the women. "He wants to know how my night's going..." Azazel looks back to Steven. "Not so great! Where are my Obols?"

Steven was about to speak up, but Azazel cuts him off.

"No! I'll answer that. You let Beth take them from you!"

Azazel gestures to the woman to pause the shoulder massage and shoos her and the other two out of the room. Once they are gone, he continues on. "So, Beth is out of hiding... I knew she would come out for him. She is absolutely obsessed with that family."

"Come on, boss, it's not so bad." The Young Man finally speaks up. "You know she'll try to stop us now. She'll come out of hiding again and when she does, that's when we'll kill her."

Azazel glares at The Young Man. "You know, when you've been top side longer than thirty seconds, I'll allow you to chime in. Until then, shut up..."

Steven jumps in to take some of the pressure off of The Young Man. "Okay, well, he is right. Beth has got to know what we're planning. Now that she has the top cop by her side, she won't hesitate to come for us."

Azazel stands up from his throne and takes a few steps closer to Steven and The Young Man. He is a looming figure. Even though Azazel is only slightly taller than both Steven and The Young Man, the immense power that he radiates has a terrifying effect on even some of the most powerful beings in the world. As he steps closer to them, they seem to shrink in size just out of pure fear.

Once he is right in front of them, with a calm but

frightening voice, he begins to speak. "Okay, Steven, you might be onto something. But you listen to me..." Azazel steps in closer. "If this plan doesn't work, you both are going back home. Do you understand me?"

With a fearful gulp both Steven and The Young Man nod in undeniable acknowledgment.

BEN'S CONCERN_
JOHN

OKAY, SO I WOKE UP IN BETH'S HOUSE, WHICH could only mean one thing — last night really happened. I was sure I just pulled a Walter and hit the bottle at Cain's Pub a bit too hard. What the hell am I going to do?

I will say, this bed is really comfortable... what is it a pillow top? Damn, I slept great.

"What time is it?" I whisper to myself.

I grab my phone to check the time. Oh, shit... Ben called. It's only 8am — he must have been worried. What do I tell him? I mean, how am I supposed to say any of this to him. He'll never believe me. I don't even know if I really believe it. Alright, I have to call him back.

He picks up on the first ring. "Well... was he there?" Ben says instead of saying hello.

"Good morning to you too, sunshine."

"Come on, John. Was he there?" Ben is in no mood for games.

I pull the phone away from my ear with hesitation. I need to proceed with caution. Since Walter has disappeared, Ben has become somewhat of a parental figure, for some reason. As if I can't take care of myself... Granted, I have let things get a bit sloppy around my office, and maybe I forget to eat from time to time, and I tend to get a bit too drunk... a bit too often. Okay, so maybe I can see why he gets a bit concerned. He's a good friend. I should cut him some slack.

I put the phone back to my ear. "Yea, Ben, he was there," I say reluctantly. I know that Ben will be upset that I didn't call him because he knows me well enough to know that I didn't just watch from my car.

"You approached him, didn't you?" Ben asks.

See what I mean...

I begin to speak, but I hesitate.

"John?" He asks as if the call dropped.

"It's complicated," I say.

Ben sighs.

"Ben, it's complicated. I can't really explain what the hell happened last night. But I'm alright. Listen, I know this won't make any sense, but I'll have to call you tomorrow and we can go over everything. I swear."

"What was so complicated? You didn't do anything stupid, did you?"

Well, I did break into the apartment of a demon, if that's what he means. In my defense, I didn't know he was a demon at the time. Maybe if I did, I would have done what Ben said and just waited in the God damn car.

"No! Of course not." I try to sound convincing. I think he bought it.

"Yea, right..." He didn't buy it. "John, I don't know what's going on with you, but just be careful. I took some time off like we talked about just to lay low, and I got a call from one of the guys at the station..." Ben has worry in his voice, more than ever before. "Chief Armers was in the bullpen again this morning. Two visits in less than twenty-four hours... something doesn't feel right."

"Was he looking for you?" I ask, knowing the answer already.

"Not just for me, but for the files I was pulling last night. He knows we're onto him. My guess is if he's willing to put himself out there like this, maybe we're uncovering something bigger than we originally thought."

"You have no idea..." I trail off.

"What do you mean?" Ben didn't understand but was curious.

"Never mind. Like I said, I'll explain more, just not over the phone. I'll call you tomorrow and we'll get together. It's too much now."

Ben groans with frustration. "Alright, well, just be

careful, John. This shit is getting serious. I'm going to call Neala over at Cain's Pub. You know she loves helping the good guys in times of trouble — maybe she'll let me hide out there until tomorrow. I know she has a room in the back for the burn out old timers who don't want to go home after a few too many."

"Good thinking. Call me if anything gets too out of hand for you." I say and hang up.

I want so badly to tell Ben everything. I always tell him everything. But how would that conversation go?

So, Ben... It turns out my Great-Great-Great-Grandfather was a world-famous demon and Fallen Angel hunter, and now I am pulled into the demon and Fallen Angel business. Oh, by who, you ask? Well, by a crazy, beautiful demon-witch that saved my life just a few hours ago. Oh, and if we don't stop them from releasing The Four Horsemen of the Apocalypse today, the world will pretty much end, and I'm the only one who can help. So, yea, you're all caught up!

You know, as I say it all like that, I sound batshit crazy...

Well, I guess I should start the day!

MORNING AFTER_
BETH

THE MORNING OF THE MAIN EVENT... AND ALL I keep thinking is what is going through John's mind? I stand in the kitchen, drinking my coffee, wondering if he slept at all or if he was up the whole night pondering the truth of the world. All the things that you think go bump in the night as a kid, all the things that adulthood inevitably ends up beating out of you, turns out to actually be walking around in the daylight. John faces the hard truth that not only were all the monsters under his bed real, but they were under his nose the whole time.

John walks into the kitchen and looks to be a bit out of it.

I'm holding my coffee cup. "Want some?" I say as I gesture with it.

"Yes, please," he says.

"Did you get any sleep?" I'm genuinely curious.

This answer could set the course for the rest of the day. If he was up all night terrified of the truth, he might not want to help me.

"Hmm... Let's see. I was in the guest room of a demon-witch — no offense—" he begins to ramble on.

"None taken," I interject almost instantly, and he continues.

"After she told me I couldn't go home because Fallen Angels and their demon minions were after me..."

Okay, so he seems pretty shaken up still.

"So, I take it you didn't sleep well."

John pauses for a moment and sips his coffee. "No, actually, I slept pretty well."

He's such an idiot... but, he had me going there — I couldn't help but laugh at that one.

"So, have you decided if you want to stick around to help me or not?"

"I have." He takes a sip of coffee. "Knowing what I know now, I can't turn my back on this. If people were to get hurt and I could have done something, anything, to stop it, I would never be able to live with myself."

I'm so happy with his decision — it's the right call to make. I can't say I never doubted him, but I had a strong feeling that he would make the right choice eventually. I'm just glad it was within enough time for us to stop Azazel and the rest of The Watchers before their big plans tonight.

"I know you're not going to be happy about this, though," John says. "I need to go to my place to grab a couple of things."

"Not alone, you're not!" I nearly cut him off.

John's eyes widen. "People don't seem to trust me lately..."

"Yea — and for a good reason! You ran half-cocked into a demon's apartment. Whether you knew about his abilities or not, you're not a cop anymore! Besides, I have clothes for you here. It's not safe for you at home. There is a change of clothes already in your room."

"How..." John looks back down the hallway toward the spare bedroom, forgetting for a second that I have magical gifts. "Never mind that. It's not just about the clothes. There's something there that you won't be able to magic up for me. I need to go."

He's definitely an idiot. I'm not happy about this, but I guess I understand. He'll most likely never be able to go back there again. Even if we are successful tonight, that doesn't mean The Watchers will go away. They'll be out for blood on both John and me.

"Fine — but I'm going with you. And you do what I say when we're there!"

"Yes, ma'am!" He says with a bit of sarcasm in his voice.

I shot him a quick dirty look. "I'm serious! I told you last night that there are different levels of demons. Well, tonight is the night that Steven and his friend will try to release The Horsemen. I would guess that they won't want us in the way. And if that is the case, they will send the strongest demons after us. They are known as The Born. They were spawned from the Mother of Demons herself."

John rolls his eyes. "I'm not sure if I like how desensitized I've already become to demons trying to kill me."

I shrug, it's never fun, but it's better than not knowing and having it happen anyways.

"Well, trust me, it's a good thing you feel that way. Now that you're in the fight, it's only going to get worse. So, it's better to roll with the punches, or spells in some cases. So, get dressed, we'll head to your place in fifteen minutes. Then, we open the armory."

John walks back to his room and mumbles under his breath. "Half-cocked... You're half-cocked..."

"What was that?!" I shout.

"Nothing!" John responds.

I shake my head and enjoy the rest of my coffee.

THE TRINKET_
JOHN

I guess this seems pretty pointless. I mean, Beth was clear that going back home would be dangerous, and quite honestly, idiotic. Well, she didn't say idiotic, but the face she made when I told her I need to go home made it seem like that's what she was thinking.

Trust me, I know that it's crazy, but what I need is priceless to me. If I'm not able to make it home again, I need to know I at least tried to get it back.

We pull up to my apartment, and we park a bit up the block. Beth is keeping a watchful eye on the street to make sure she doesn't spot anyone suspicious. She tells me she thinks everything is clear. She saved my life and gave me a place to stay — I feel like I'm in good hands with her.

"Okay, once you get in, you won't have a lot of time," Beth says, as she begins rifling through a small satchel backpack she is carrying. "Enter through the front door, and if anyone is watching, they won't think you're onto them. Then, when you have what you need, quickly leave through the fire escape. I'll be in the alley with the car."

"Wait — you're not coming in with me? You can just magic them away!"

I don't think Beth enjoyed my comment. She gives me a dirty look... and even though — again — this is not the right time, even her dirty looks are cute. Wait... no, John, hold it together...

"Okay, first of all, can you stop using my magic as a verb?" Beth asks.

"Sorry..." I say playfully to make her smile.

It didn't work... she rolls her eyes and continues on.

"Second, if they send The Born, we need to get out in a hurry. I can take on one or two, but if it's more than that, we're both dead, or worse."

"They're really that bad?" She has me on my heels.

"Yes." She says bluntly.

"Wonderful."

When I initially wanted to come back to the apartment, I wasn't expecting this. Of course, after Beth explained that they would be looking for us, and that she would need to accompany me, I thought she would protect me again like she did at Steven's place. I mean, when you have your own super-witch on your side, what can go wrong?! However, I wasn't expecting her to be afraid of anything, especially the way she came storming into Steven's apartment last night. I guess this is just my new demon-hunting life now — nope, still weird to say.

Beth finally finds what she was looking for in her backpack.

"Don't worry, that's why I have this." She pulls out a small glass vial from her backpack. "A friend of mine made it for me. It's a potion. If anything happens to you in there, throw it at the ground as hard as you can."

"What is it?" I immediately ask as I'm a bit hesitant.

"Think of it as a demon flashbang — just with an extra kick," Beth says as she hands me the potion. "It won't kill any of The Born, just slow them down a bit."

I grab it and put it in my pocket. "Well, if we have this, then why can't you come in?"

"Because it is strong enough to kill me..." She says without hesitation.

"Oh..."

"Just remember — take the fire escape, and I'll see you in the alley."

"Got it!" I say as I head to my apartment.

I carefully look over my shoulder as to not give away that I'm onto anyone. As I was just about to walk in the front door, I notice that Beth has driven away. I'm on my own from here on out. I wave to Pete, the owner of the newsstand, on my way in, as I would any other day, and I'm through the door.

I'm in the building and I don't see anyone that seems out of place, so I head to my unit. I make it to my front door and, with caution, I enter.

It's strange, it was only yesterday that I was here last, but it feels as if it has been years. So much has happened since I was here last that I don't even remember who the person was that lived here.

The place is messy and nearly empty. That's not me. I look around the room and I remember who I once was — before I became consumed by Walter's case. Before it was all I could see. Before I became a terrible friend and brother to Ben and left my career. I was a different person then. I know that Walter would have done everything in his power to find me if I were the one who went missing, but I think I might have taken it too far. I look at this apartment and see the files scattered across my desk — just one of the very few pieces of furniture within this place. Then, I recap the events that transpired between yesterday and today, and I think of how small of an impact I had on the world compared to what Beth has done with her life after going rogue and turning against Hell. I know this is a bit off-topic, but I bet that's a pretty cool story! I should really ask her one of these days. Back to what I was saying — I really need to put things into a better perspective and get my life back together. I don't know if I like who I've become.

Okay, I've been standing around long enough... I need to get what I came for and get out.

Along with the, let's just say, limited amenities that come with my humble abode, there is a bookshelf in the corner of the apartment. I walk up to the bookshelf to grab what I'm here for when I'm suddenly struck by my past.

My bookshelf doubles as my knick-knack and picture shelf. There are some pictures from nights at Cain's Pub with old friends, friends that I've let down over the past as of late. It just reminds me all over again who I don't want to be. I see Walter, Neala, Ben, and myself all smiling together. Along with a picture of just Walter and me from my Academy Graduation — he was so proud to be there with me that day.

Right next to that picture is what I came for — a leather flip-top box with gold trim. The box isn't important, but what's inside of it is.

I open it and pull out a gold pocket watch. It's crazy to think this one little thing can mean so much to me. I flip it around and read the engraving on the back.

"John, I am so proud of you. Walter"

It was a gift that Walter gave me when I graduated from the Academy. Over the last two years, I would look at this watch to give myself hope.

Hope that Walter was still out there. Hope that I would find him. Now, I'm hoping it becomes my good luck charm during these insane times.

I leave the box but put the watch in my pocket.

I spent way too much time here, Beth is waiting. I need to go.

I head for the window to leave through the fire escape. As I'm opening it, someone kicks in my front door. Son of bitch, of course... I had to waste time reminiscing.

Four large men storm in my front door — The Born, I presume.

I'm guessing that because these men are not like anything I've seen before. They are giants among men, well, among demons, I should say. They are towering in stature and barrel-chested. Their arms are like tree trunks and their legs seem to be the size of my waist. Honestly, if one of them punched me, I'm sure it would go straight through me.

All four are standing near my doorway, staring at me. I stop dead in my tracks right at the window.

"Oh, hey... How's it going, fellas?" I say, jokingly, trying to mask my fear and also praying I don't piss myself.

I know I don't stand a chance, but I thought if I acted unafraid, I could catch them off-guard and make my getaway.

According to Beth, demons pass for humans, but The Born couldn't even pass for bodybuilders. I think she got her facts wrong. Either that or my fear is making me see things. Yea — let's go with that.

I immediately turn and try to leave, but I don't even get one limb through the window before one of The Born grabs the back of my shirt. He pulls me back inside and effortlessly throws me clean across the room.

My apartment is not that big, but I can tell you it is not small enough that I would have ever expected to have been thrown from one end to the next. Luckily for me included in the limited furniture I have is a couch along the same wall I was thrown into. So, after I made a John-sized dent in the wall, I fell *gently* onto the couch.

After I hit the couch, I quickly attempt to reach for the potion Beth gave me that's in my pocket, but I feel my body jolt. The Born are at the other end of my room, but yet, something is definitely pulling me. The feeling is the same as it was last night at Steven's apartment.

The immense fear I have at this moment is causing the world around me to move in slow motion. It's both a wonderful and terrifying thing all at the same time. I'm able to see what is happening to me - *a wonderful thing*. But at the same time, I'm able to see what's happening to me... *a terrifying thing*.

One of The Born has his arm raised in the air, while the others stand there and watch as he telekinetically lifts me in the air and bounces me off the ceiling, then the floor, and back to the ceiling. I finally hit the floor one last time and I feel the release of the pull. Now, I know I'm free.

This won't do anything, but maybe it'll throw them off their guard just enough, so I reach for my gun. I draw, aim, and fire round after round until I hear the click of the empty magazine.

"Oh... fuck..." I say with a sigh of defeat.

It wasn't until the click of the empty gun that I realize, unlike The Young Man, The Born weren't fazed at all by the gunshots.

They shake them off, and there aren't even wounds that need to heal. It's almost as if their skin is made of Kevlar.

I shout as they begin to walk toward me. "Wait! Wait!"

They stop and look at each other. One of them speaks up. He has a deep voice; it was gravelly and almost hard to understand.

"What?"

This is my chance to buy time, to stall them and reach for the potion. I just need to say something, anything, to get them to look away from me for the briefest of moments. It's the only way I could get my hand back in my pocket.

"Look, you want something from me, right? Otherwise, you would have already killed me. So, how about we just skip the hard part and I go with you?"

The Born begin to look at each other, contemplating the idea. Almost as if they were upset that if they took me up on the offer, they would be bothered that they could not continue throwing me around.

As soon as they take their eyes off me, I reach for my pocket and pull out the glass vial that Beth gave me. I throw it as hard as I can at the floor near their feet.

A giant blast shoots out from the tiny vial, and The Born are hurled against wall. The blast sends only The Born flying and leaves me completely unaffected. This gives me the space to sprint to the window on the other side of the apartment. I glance back at them, expecting to see them unconscious, but I was mistaken. Flashbang with a kick... I should have asked more questions.

As I glance back, I see each of The Born struggling to stand as their charred bodies are now slowly starting to heal. Whatever was in this potion was not allowing their bodies to heal like a typical wound would on a demon. It was also slowing them down and seemed to be muting their powers, so I was free from their telekinesis — for now. However, they were still able to walk after me — slowly, but still walking.

I got to the fire escape and peered down the thirteen floors I still need to run down to get to the alley — Beth is there waiting for me. Finally, a win!

I make it two floors and notice that The Born have slowly made their way out of the window. Their bodies are still charred but nowhere near as bad as they were. They are healing and they are getting faster. It's only a matter of time until their powers are back.

I begin yelling for Beth. She can help me — she has to help me.

"Beth!!!"

But there is no answer.

"Beth!!!"

Still no answer... What the fuck is she doing in there?

I look back over my shoulder, and The Born are catching up to me. I'm on the 8th floor, and I'm not sure if I can make it.

Everyone has thought about how they would die, even if they don't want to admit it. Would it be that time you drank too much in college and your friend dared you to do something stupid? Would it be when you're old on your death bed and you get to say, 'Come closer, come closer' and then not say anything and leave someone guessing... that would be fun. A little morbid? Yea, I know. Out of all the ways you can think to go, running down a fire escape being chased by charred demons spawned straight from the Mother of Demons is not one of the ways I would have pictured it... Son of a bitch!

THE ESCAPE_
BETH

I HOPE JOHN WILL BE OKAY IN THERE. No, I know he will be! If things get rough, he has that potion. That's why I couldn't go in. That thing could really hurt The Born, but it could also kill me if he ends up using it.

The fact of the matter is The Watchers plan is too important this time around to leave anything to chance. They know that John is the key to stopping them and they know I will stop at nothing to take them down.

As I wait in the alley, I begin to think about John quite a bit. This morning, I thought he would have been in much rougher shape, but he seemed to have handled it pretty well. Hell, he was even joking a bit. It was nice to see him laughing again...

There was so much more I wanted to tell him last night — about his past, about his family, about me. I knew that I dropped so much information on him, that I would scare him away if I let out anymore, especially with what I really wanted to tell him. That I had been the one keeping him safe all these years. That this morning was not the first time I had heard him laugh, or that the diner was not the first time that I had sat just a table away from him — it was just the first time he had noticed me.

After years of being on the run from Beings more powerful than he can imagine, I have gotten excellent at hiding in plain sight. However, last night at the diner, I was off my game. I was too busy thinking about what might be going on with Azazel and the rest of The Watchers and that damn tomb. Then, I look up and I could see his eyes looking at mine. I wasn't sure what to do. I thought my cover was blown. That's why I had to get the hell out of there.

I would have come clean with him sooner, but I knew if he didn't see the truth with his own eyes, I would have just been some crazy woman ranting about the end of the world to him. He needed to be face to face with real evil before I could tell him why I had been watching over him, like I am now.

With all of this in mind, I soon realize that it has been some time that he has been in there. I hope he knows this isn't a time for him to be taking a walk down memory lane. Well, while I wait, I might as well listen to some music.

I turn on the radio and flip through the stations.

"Nothing. Garbage. Nothing."

That's when I hear it.

"I love this song!"

I immediately start using the steering wheel as a drum set and singing along to the radio.

"Mmmbop, ba duba dop!"

As I'm just getting into the song, that's when I hear it — the muffled sounds of panic.

"Beth!" It's John screaming.

I open the car door and look up at the fire escape. I can see him several floors up, and not far behind are the charred bodies of The Born gaining their speed back — and their strength.

I yell, "Oh shit — John, run!"

"I'm trying!" He says, sounding a bit upset. I'm assuming this wasn't the first time John has yelled for me. I was too deep in thought.

"I can try to hold them off once you're closer. I don't want to hurt you, though." I shout back up to him.

John begins to jump down each flight of stairs, but there are still five more to go and The Born are gaining on him.

"Goddammit, just do it!" he shouts again.

I shake my head, knowing he's going to regret this. "Okay, but I warned you!"

I gather all the strength I have for a spell to fight back against The Born. Luckily, they are already wounded, but it will still need to be strong enough to stop a freight train to faze them.

I have the power I need, so I use both hands to thrust the energy out of my body and shout, "INSPIRATIONE."

The force from the spell throws all four of The Born up several flights of stairs and through the wall, landing them into one of John's downstairs neighbors — they will not be happy with him.

However, the force also throws John from the fire escape, and it lands him directly on top of his truck. He bounces from the impact and fell on the cement of the alleyway.

After landing on the ground, words slowly falls from his mouth. "Son of a bitch..."

I run to his side. "Are you okay?" I kneel down to check to see how he's doing and I put my hand on his chest. He looks up at me, and we pause for a moment.

After the pause, I remove my hand, and he speaks. "Yea... Let's just get the hell out of here."

I help him up slowly and we look up at the apartment. Fire is forming from where The Born re-entered the building. It looks like John isn't going home any time soon.

We start walking to the truck, and John looks at me. "Hey, were you listening to Hanson while I was running for my life?"

I'm a caught off guard a bit. "What?! No! Shut up..."

I help him into the passenger seat, and he mumbles out in tune, "Mmmbop..." in a mocking tone.

I give him a dirty look and he just says, "Hey, it's a good song!"

I shake my head, and smirk. I close the door. Like John said — we need to get the hell out of here.

THE VAULT_

BETH

Without a doubt, that was one of the
closest calls I have had in a long time — and I wasn't
even in the room. I can't even imagine what's going on
in John's mind.

I look at him, sitting on the couch, gazing at the
floor in disbelief of the events that just unfolded
before his eyes. A few scrapes and some bruises
beginning to form, and I'm afraid to ask him what
really happened in there. I fear that if he relives it all,
it will make him question the decision he made this
morning to stick this out. He is stronger than he
realizes. He was made for this life, even if he doesn't
know it yet.

He slowly looks up from the floor. "Well, it looks
like I really can't go back to my apartment now."

I could tell he was trying to make a joke out of it,
but deep down he was terrified. At that moment, he

was vulnerable. I want to sit next to him and comfort him. Are we there yet? Am I his friend, or am I just the woman screaming 'end times' in his ear? In twenty-four hours, we have gone through more than anyone else has — I'm sure of it. But does that bind two people? Or does that just make us survivors?

Of course, throughout the years, I've grown to care about his safety. However, he doesn't know that. And of course, there is an attraction — how could there not be? But that's not important. I honestly just want to know that he's okay. I just need to ease into this. If I push too hard, I could scare him off.

"I'm sorry, John. Did you get everything you needed at least?"

John nods his head to say 'yes.' He pulls a pocket watch out from his pocket. A small smile falls over his face — a gentle smile. He's still terrified from the day he just had, but this watch just brightened his face up. He rubs his fingers over the engraving on the back of it.

Without taking his eyes off the watch, he says, "I'm surprised this held up in the fall."

"What is it?" I say as I sit down on the couch next to him.

John looks up from the watch and explains.

"Walter gave this to me when I graduated from the Academy. He was the only family I had back then. My mom was gone, my aunt had died from a stroke when I was only seventeen, so it was just the

two of us by that time. He was always there for me."
John takes a breath to keep from choking up, then put
the watch back in his pocket. "So, I guess we should
get over to the armory and start prepping for tonight,
huh?"

I skip past the remarks about the watch, as I know
John isn't looking to dwell on it.

"Yea, we should get ready. However, the armory
is much closer than you would think."

John gives me a strange look, curious as to where
it may be.

"You see, after your grandfather died, I wanted to
make sure it was always close by. That way, the next
Gideon had quick access to it should they need it."

I stand up from the couch and head to a bookcase
along the wall in the living room. I slide back several
fake books to reveal a keypad, to John's surprise, and I
enter a security code: 0414.

"So, to keep it close, I built my home over it."

After the code is entered, a door unlocks,
allowing the bookcase to swing open and reveal a
staircase.

John slowly stands up from the couch. He's in
shock that there is a hidden passageway behind my
bookcase — but only for a moment.

"I don't know why I'm shocked. It's you, of course,
you have a secret room in your house."

"It's not just a room," I say, as I gesture for him to
follow me.

I begin walking down the stairs, and he follows.

"I built these townhouses about fifteen years after the Chicago Fire and have lived here ever since. However, this... bunker, I guess you can call it, was here for some time before that. I originally just had a small home here and kept myself hidden for some time."

We make it down the flight of stairs, and I turn on the lights to reveal much more than just a room.

What can be seen is a steel wall with a vault door running along the left side of the stairwell that stretches the length of the home. To the right of the stairwell is wide open space with tables and bookshelves stocked with grimoires, potions, and loose sheets of paper to track new spells. This stretches on for what would be two of the townhouses — from the outside, of course.

"What is this place?" John asks, in awe.

"I thought you were done being surprised?" I laugh.

"Yea, that was before I walked into Narnia..." He looks around the space, taking it all in. He is like a kid in a candy store.

"This is where I spend most of my time. I call it The Vault. Everything over there," I point to the grimoires, spells and potions, "Is where I like to 'magic things up' as some might say..." I roll my eyes at him.

He grins — I kind of like joking with him. I haven't had anyone around to joke with in so long.

Most of my friendships always feel so transactional — something about this one is more substantial. It could be because I've been keeping an eye on him without him knowing for a while... I will need to tell him that eventually... shit. Okay... moving on.

"I have all my grimoires, which are just my spell books. I also have potions, and just some other spells I work on. And everything over there," I point to the steel wall, "Is the armory! It's locked and will only open for you. Luckily, my friend left me the spell and I will be able to open it for you!"

John gives me a strange look, "So, who is this mysterious friend of yours?"

"Oh, don't worry, you'll meet her soon enough! But right now, we need to get this door open. I'll be honest, though, it's not going to be fun."

"Why is that?" John asks curiously.

"Well..." I pause. "I'm going to need just a little bit of your blood," I say in a slight whisper to lighten the mood.

"Yea, I'm out." John begins to walk toward the stairwell.

I grab his sleeve and laugh. "No! It's nothing crazy! It's only from your finger. Think of it as a paper cut."

"That's all?" He asks, clearly unhappy about it.

"That's all," I say to reassure him with my hand still on his arm.

"Okay then, let's just get it over with." John sticks out his hand, turns his head and closes his eyes tight.

I put my hand to my face and shake my head. "Big baby..."

I laugh as I walk over to a table where I keep some of my grimoires.

"It's a bit more complicated than that. It's a blood spell." John opens his eyes and looks at me, and I continue on. "So, it's not like what you've seen me do so far. I need to prepare a bit. Why don't you go grab few of those candles and a piece of chalk, and you can help me set up?"

I point to a table behind me, and John walks over to grab everything I need. I pick up the grimoire left for me by my friend, and I walk back to the armory door, and John follows timidly behind. He's like a scared little puppy — it's kind of cute.

I move a small table in place to hold the grimoire and find the spell I need.

"Okay, I'll take that chalk now, please."

I take the chalk and draw a pentagram on the floor directly in front of the armory door. It's large enough for John to stand in the center of it.

"What's that for?" John asks with fear in his voice.

"The armory will only open for the Gideon family bloodline. This pentagram serves as a binding key. If something were to happen to you, the armory seals back up until the next member of the Gideon family opens the lock. This guarantees that no one can kill you and steal what's inside."

"Oh, well, that sounds nice... I think..." John is oddly reassured.

"Okay, now, I need you to place a candle at each of the five points, please."

John places each candle around the pentagram and then steps back toward me.

"Do you need me to light them?" he asks.

"No need," I say, and then I raise both hands in the air and say, "INCENSA."

All at once, all five candles light at the same time.

John tenses up, but I place my hand on his back and he relaxes again.

"I need you to step into the center of the pentagram now. I promise it won't be bad, okay?"

"Okay." He's cautious, but he steps in.

I was about to follow him in with a dagger for the blood portion of the spell when I could see his hesitation.

"Do you trust me?"

John looks in my eyes. I could see and even feel his fear, but he still held my gaze. Someone he just met is now walking toward him with a dagger — and I'm not ashamed to admit it — in what could amount to a creepy dungeon. He has every reason not to trust me, but yet something in his eyes is just so calm at this moment. His body is shaking and he's afraid, I understand that, but his eyes are strong.

When asked if he trusted me, without a single twitch in his voice, he replied, "Yes."

I didn't say anything else. I just follow in after him and slowly reach for his hand without breaking eye contact.

"Just breathe," I say.

I finally take my eyes off his and look down at his hands - which are no longer shaking. I could feel him staring at me, not at the dagger, not at his hand that I'm about to stab into, but at me. I keep my focus, and with the tip of the dagger, I make a tiny prick into his pointer finger. He doesn't flinch and I can still feel his eyes on me.

I turn his hand over and squeeze his finger to drip several drops of blood on the chalk outline onto the floor beneath us. I turn his hand back around, place my other hand over the cut, and look back at him. His eyes have not left the spot they were before. I could feel him tracing my face with his eyes. Normally, I would be confused, and maybe a bit uncomfortable, however, this time, I enjoy it.

I meet his gaze, and in a soft voice, I speak, "MALUM ULTRA."

With those words, the cut on John's hand is gone.

"You can heal people?" John is astounded.

I'm still holding onto John's hand, but at this point, he reaches up to grip my other hand as well. I can't tell if I'm overthinking this. I feel as if we've been standing here for days, but I don't want it to end.

I feel the touch of both of his hands on mine, and I know this is exactly what I want — yet I'm afraid.

"Only little wounds," I say, thinking I should begin to pull away — but goddammit, I don't want to...

I look back up to see his eyes staring right back at me. He smiles, and it actually makes his eyes brighten a bit. The wider his smile grows, the deeper the dimple gets on the right side of his face. For the most part, it hides perfectly under his 5 o'clock shadow but now it's more prominent than ever. After all the time I've spent protecting him, of course, I have thought about the attraction. However, it wasn't until tonight that I began to feel a genuine connection — but is it wrong? Is he only connecting to me because I saved him? Once we finish our task tonight, will he be on his way? There will be so much more work to do, but will he still want to do it? And will he want to still work with me? I've spent so many years working from the shadows, I don't know if I can come out of hiding now only to be hurt in more ways than one. Maybe I should pull away... just to be safe.

I've gotten so far off-topic, I almost forgot what I was telling him...

"It takes so much energy that if the injury is near-fatal, it could potentially kill me." I start to pull my hand away — it's the right thing to do. Maybe the best time to do it. "So, don't go dying on me!" I make a slight joke to break the tension.

John didn't look very happy about me pulling my hand away. Maybe he feels the same after all... But I can't risk it.

"I won't!" He says jokingly, trying to save face.

John's blood, which is now working its way through the chalk outline, causes the flames to react and they shine brighter for just a moment before the light gleams to its usual glow.

"So, now what?" John asks.

"Now comes the hard part. Just stay in the center. Okay?" I say as I brush his arm for one last touch. I'm regretting how soon I let go of his hand.

"Okay..." He says with hesitation.

I stand in front of the table, holding my grimoire, and get ready for the spell. I glance at John one last time, the fear is back in his eyes, but I can tell he is trying to hide it from me.

"You'll be okay, I promise."

"I trust you." He says, and with those words, this warmth washes over me. It's been so long since I've had this connection. I smile to let John know things will be okay.

"I'm going to start the spell now, so just relax and don't move."

He nods, and I begin.

I take a deep breath and begin speaking slowly.

"SI SANGUIS TRIBUTO."

The candles begin to burn brighter, and John looks around the room. I can sense the fear, I want to tell him to keep calm, but I can't break my concentration, so I speak again, as the spell is not yet complete.

I repeat the spell again, this time with more power.

"SI SANGUIS TRIBUTO."

The chalk outline on the floor begins to light up as if it were being electrocuted. The color of the chalk sparks red over and over. Now, the flames again spark up brighter and brighter. John tenses up but remains strong.

I repeat the spell one last time with even more power. I am nearly straining my voice.

"SI SANGUIS TRIBUTO!"

The pentagram's chalk outline turns a solid blood-red color for just a moment and the flame on the candles spark almost to the ceiling.

Then, the flames burn out within an instant and the blood-red color turns back to white. Everything is back to normal.

"What in the actual fuck was all that?" John asks and looks at me in shock. "Did it work? The chalk is white again. Did... did I do something wrong?"

"Oh no, it worked! The chalk is imbued with the spell, and now it cannot be washed away. We won't need to do this spell every time, so don't worry!" I say, knowing that will make John happy.

"Thank god!" he says with a chuckle, and a sigh of relief.

"This," I point to the pentagram, "as I said, is your key."

John turns to stare at the door. I step forward to stand at his side.

LOVER BOY_
JOHN

HAVE I BEEN STARING TOO LONG? SHIT, I THINK I've been staring too long. I just can't take my eyes off of her.

While standing in the — pentagram — I can't believe I'm talking about this like it's a normal thing, I'm terrified. But after she took a step inside and I felt her close to me, suddenly there was this incredible calm that fell over me as soon as she looked at me. I was safe. I don't know, maybe I'm being crazy. I always do this, I think something might be there, then I hesitate at the last second and never act on it.

Why would a woman like Beth be interested in someone like me, anyways? She is incredible, and I haven't been on my A-game lately...

I know I don't know much about her, but there's just something that gives me this confidence when

I'm with her. It makes me feel like I'm my old self again, the normal John.

When she stepped into the pentagram and took my hand, we locked eyes and I was hooked. I couldn't think of anything else, and my fear was gone.

Her eyes... What's not to say? They were hazel, but then as the candlelight flickered I could begin to see more of the green, then even a hint of orange — not gold, but orange. I wasn't sure if it was just a reflection of the light, but it was in there. It was deep in her eyes, but I wasn't going to miss even the slightest color.

She looked at me and I wasn't afraid. For the first time in almost twenty-four hours, I was not afraid. I'm not sure if it was because she was holding my hand or just because we were making eye contact for what seemed to have lasted days, but I felt at ease — minus my shaky hands, of course... I hope she didn't notice that.

I do my best to steady my hands and my body. Even though I'm not afraid, I think the rest of my body is catching up to what my mind and heart are feeling in this moment.

She finally breaks eye contact and looks down at my hand. As she looks down, the scent from her hair sweeps into my nose and it is intoxicating. There is not a single thing about this woman in which I can find a flaw. Between her strength and beauty, I just feel struck by her.

She draws a dagger. She's holding it to my pointer finger and slices — I don't flinch. I'm staying strong and I've stopped shaking, but on the inside I probably sound like a toddler who has been teething for a month straight.

Beth is keeping her eyes focused on my hand as the blood begins to pool at my fingertip. I still cannot take my eyes off of her. I look at her face, trying to memorize every inch. I fear that after we complete our task tonight I will never be this close to her again, and I want to remember this feeling. The feeling of being this close to her. Maybe it's strange, I mean, I hardly know her. However, something seems familiar. I knew when I saw her at the diner she stood out to me, but it wasn't until I made eye contact with her just a moment ago that I felt as if we had been bonded in ways I cannot begin to explain. Strange — I know.

Yet, here I am, standing in this fucking dungeon — I won't tell her that because I don't want to make her feel bad, but she really built herself a torture shack down here. But being down here doesn't seem to bother me. Of course, I'm a bit on edge, she has me standing in the center of a pentagram with candles she lit using only her hands. Not to mention, she just slit open my finger with a large dagger — so there is that part of it. However, I look at her, and I don't know... it all just fades away. Have you ever felt that way about a person you just met? I haven't before, that's why I'm asking, because I don't know what the hell it all means.

And I know I'm rambling, but my god, I can't control myself.

She turns my hand over and drips just a few drops of blood onto the chalk outline on the floor beneath our feet. I still don't take my eyes off her.

I study her. Her medium-blonde hair, which almost seems lighter with the candles burning; the light color to her skin brings out the smallest freckles around her petite and slightly upturned nose; her lips... my god, her lips... which I have been spending every ounce of energy I have on fighting myself to not kiss. The last thing I need is to piss her off and have her send me sailing through the air or breaking me in half for reading the wrong signals.

Beth turns my hand back around. She places her other hand directly above the slice in my finger, gazes at me, and speaks in almost a whisper.

"MALUM ULTRA."

I don't look down, but I can feel what she has done. The cut on my finger is gone. I could feel the skin close on my finger and it's absolutely unbelievable. I truly thought I'd seen everything up to this point, but now... now, I have seen it all.

"You can heal people?" I say astounded.

That's when I think it's the perfect time to show her how happy I feel next to her. I just hope she feels the same.

I reach out with my other hand and take the hand she used to heal me. She was holding one of my hands, now, I am holding one of hers. I run my thumb softly along the side of her hand.

I smile. She smiles back. Her soft lips part slightly, but only for a moment. Hesitation? Does she feel the same? Is she afraid? Or is she just being polite? Damn, John, you went too far...

She explains how she can only heal small wounds, that it's harmful to her. Then she begins to pull her hands away. I try my hardest not to show that it saddens me, but I'm sure Beth already knows what I'm feeling. If she felt it too, she wouldn't have pulled her hands back. Maybe it's not meant to be...

THE ARMORY_
JOHN

BETH AND I STAND BEFORE THE ARMORY DOOR. I'm hesitant to open it. I don't know what to expect. A giant pile of scrap metal, or maybe another dagger or two for Beth to poke me with? I honestly don't know. I just hope whatever it is, there is enough of it to help us tonight.

All I know for sure is that Beth is confident. She knows with certainty that whatever is behind this door will stop The Watchers pursuit. As far as I know, she hasn't been in this room since my Great-Great-Great-Grandfather died a century ago. Now that I think about it, that's probably not true. She mentioned that this armory was spelled to open for anyone within the Gideon bloodline. She has, more than likely, worked with others in my family but just hasn't told me yet. I shouldn't be so naive to think I'm the first to stumble onto this.

Either way, I've spent enough time standing here. I can tell Beth is wondering what the hell is taking me so long because she's looking at me funny...

"Oh, sorry, I got a little nervous," I say to break the awkward tension.

She just shakes her head as I reach for the giant handle of the door.

The armory wall is like a giant bank vault. The handle is a steel wheel. Turning it slightly releases the locking rods, allowing it to open. I pull the door open, and we take a step inside.

I am in absolute amazement.

"Jesus tap-dancing Christ."

"What the fuck was that?" Beth asks, confused and looking at me like I was an idiot.

"Honestly, I have no idea — I just have never seen anything like this before." I am in shock with how stupid I just sounded, but also with what I was seeing.

I look around the armory, which stretches out the rest of the length of Beth's house. Her vault, as she called it, was only two of her homes. This was the other three - and they aren't small homes.

Tables are lining the armory, as close as can be, while still allowing enough room to squeeze by. Some of the tables were neatly organized with knives, swords, and daggers — any form of blade you can think of really.

Other tables had stockpiles of ammunition. Each

table has corresponding firearms to match the ammo — everything from pistols to long-guns to fucking rocket-launchers!

The N.R.A would be in Heaven right now if they could see this room. It's a good thing Beth doesn't work with them... Who knows what their people would do with this kind of firepower.

Then, along one wall, there are giant weapons, things I couldn't even begin to name even if I wanted to. On the other wall are larger swords that are more pristine — I could tell some of them had real work put into them.

It was at that moment I realized she been in this armory more recently than I initially thought. There are even tarps covering random piles of steel on the floor that has yet to be forged. Some of the tables have quite a bit of dust covering the weapons. However, most of what we are seeing upfront has been wiped down, with only a small amount of dust on it.

This room clearly does not have much ventilation, so it would take some time for the dust to gather here. It was not long ago that she had been here, but which one of my family members lost their life to lock this place back up? I need to know that story, but right now, we have work to do.

I begin walking further through the armory, still in disbelief.

"When you told me that you had steel from the

Chicago Fire, I thought I would be walking into a garbage dump. This is beyond anything I could have imagined."

"And it's all yours!" Beth says with a smile.

"No..." I stop to look at her. "It's all ours. We are doing this together. I wouldn't even know of any of this if it weren't for you." I pause in thought. "Hell, I would probably be dead if it weren't for you."

Beth speaks up in a serious tone. "You know, I haven't really thanked you for not running away from all of this when you had the chance. It takes a lot to run into this head-on."

She takes a step toward me, but then she immediately pulls back.

Then, in typical Beth fashion, she tries to break the tension with what I guess is her trying to be funny. "Plus, we get all this cool stuff!"

She grabs a broad ax from the wall by the handle, most likely not realizing the head of it would be much heavier than anticipated and drops it immediately.

She scares the crap out of me.

She stumbles to pick it up and put it back up on the wall as I chuckle to myself.

"Yea, seriously, this is all pretty cool! I can't believe you've had all of this under your house..." I nearly cut myself off. "Actually, what am I saying? It's you. Of course, I can believe it. I can believe pretty much anything now."

Beth rolls her eyes at me. "Well, I think it's a good idea if we arm up and get ready!"

"Yea, I should get some ammo!" I say and head to one of the tables.

Beth heads to a wall of swords, and without looking at anything else, she immediately slings a jet-black duel-back-strap over her shoulders.

She picks up a 28" Katana sword with a white rope grip and looks at it for just a moment. She looks at it with a face that says, 'I've missed you.'

On the blade is a pattern. I guess it would be hard to call it a pattern, as there is nothing orderly about it. It would almost be safe to call it a smudge, and it runs along the edge of the blade. It's char marks from when the steel was scorched by the Hellfire from the blaze in 1871. It's the mark that imbues it with its energy.

Looking through the armory, every single piece of Hellfire Forged steel, whether it's laying on a table or hanging on the wall, has a similar mark. The blades have their own unique marks running along the edges, and the ammunition has its own marks scattered around the bullet.

Beth takes her Katana and slides it into the first slot of her strap. Then, she reaches for the 20" Wakizashi blade that was next to it. Exact same white rope grip, almost exact same blade, just shorter — the counterpart to her 28" Katana, what you can call her quick-draw weapon.

I can't stop walking up and down the armory; it's just out of this world. Maybe it's because I wasn't expecting to see even a fraction of this when the door opened. I'm in such shock. I mean, where did she get all of this from?! I know we don't have time to act like a kid in a toy store, so I need to just get what I need for tonight, and then we can go. But maybe Beth will let me raid the place a little later — some of these things might really help me hunt for Walter.

So, I walk to one of the tables to get some of this *magic* ammo — please don't tell Beth I used the word magic like that — and while I do that, something on the wall next to me catches my eye.

"Are these my initials?" I ask Beth, who is now ready and just waiting for me to finish up.

"Well, technically, they're your grandfather's initials. That was his sword — it was one of the first things we forged. His name was also John Gideon, but he preferred to go by Jonathan."

I take it off the wall, pull it from its leather sheath, and look it over a bit more. It's a 26" Viking Battle Sword with an ivory and brass handle. On the ivory is "J.G." in gold leaf. It's a double-edged sword, and along both edges, even toward the center of the blade leading to the point, is the same charred pattern that can be found on everything else.

Beth speaks up, so I take my eyes off the sword and look at her. "Jonathan loved that sword. I think

158 / CARL NOVAKOVICH

it's fitting for you to carry it with you tonight." She smiles at me.

The sheath is meant to be worn as a cross-body carry as it's a shorter blade. So, I throw it over my head and wear it on my right shoulder. I slide the sword in the sheath behind my back.

A POSSIBLE FAREWELL_
BETH

My Dear Friend,

If you do not hear from me by tomorrow, then John and I did not make it.

I'm leaving this note in The Vault because I know you will check in on us. If the armory is still open, it means they've captured us and kept us alive - but it won't be for long. I need you to promise you will keep them from the contents inside. Swear on your family. I know I can't hear you say it, but I know that you will.

If I do not make it, there are a few things I want to say.

You've been the only friend I've had over these past years. For that, I'm grateful. You cannot understand the pressure I've been under since 1871, knowing that this day would come. Even more so when I learned that their power was slowly oozing from the tomb.

I have been thinking lately — countless people walk directly above the tomb every day and have no clue of the evil that lurks below them. If only they knew...

People come from all over to visit the Water Tower Place, not realizing that right across the street at the Pumping Station is where the world may very well come to an end one day.

I hope John and I are strong enough to stop what's coming, but you know just as well as I, that it's a tall order.

The thing is, I have spent the last century and a half preparing for this day and I am still terrified.

However, I rely on that fear because it's the best motivation. Fear reminds us that we still have something worth losing.

If this evil is released, we may very well lose the war, and this world will be theirs. But remember what I've always said — this world is still worth fighting for. As flawed as it is, we cannot give up. We've come so far and there is still so much more we can accomplish.

So, I have one more favor to ask.

If this is the end for me, I need you to fight. If John and I lose this battle tonight, keep fighting. They believe we are the only ones who will stand up against them. They feel no one is strong enough. But they have not met you.

Promise me, if this is the end of us, let it be the beginning of the revolution. Let it start with us.

John and I will take the first watch; whether we succeed or not, they will not win.

Your Friend,
Beth May

THE WALK UP_
BETH

WALKING UP TO THE WATER TOWER PUMPING
Station is a frightening thing. I feel as if I'm more on
edge than John right now. Maybe that's because I
know what to expect; I've faced what's in that tomb
before. John is still fresh to all of this; he may be in
denial or maybe he is just masking it well. It's tough
to tell though. As I'm doing my best to hold it
together for his sake, he seems to be having a blast
with a sword on his back — he won't stop playing
with the God damn thing. I swear he's like a child
sometimes.

"Would you cut it out!" I say in a half-yell, half-
whisper tone, as to not give away that we're here just
in case anyone is waiting outside for us. "You're going
to cut yourself."

"Sorry, I have just never walked around with a
really cool sword on my back before."

See what I mean... a damn child.

"You know, speaking of weapons. I get why I have them, but why do you need them? Can't you just use your magic?" He asks.

I shake my head.

"Sometimes, it's faster to use a weapon. If I'm fighting The Born, I can't always compete against them as my powers aren't as strong as theirs. I mean, I had to basically drop your apartment on them to stop them earlier. Plus, you can't tell me these swords aren't totally badass."

"Oh, you definitely look really cool! I was just wondering."

I knew he would like that one. He's a dork. Eh, he's kind of cute, though... Dammit, Beth, keep it together!

"So, what's the plan here?" John asks, now being more serious.

"Well, you're not going to like it, but to be honest, I'm kind of winging it."

John stops dead in his tracks.

"Wait — what?" He is really not happy about that.

"Well, I know what we need to do! The problem is, I just don't know how many demons we will run into. There is a good chance we will only see Steven and his buddy down there. But we will need to be careful because..." I hesitate and then mumble under my breath, "They may have brought back up."

"Back up!?" John says, a bit too loud.

"Oh, good, so you heard that."

"Back up, like those big bastards that attacked me in my apartment?" John is getting a bit anxious.

"Possibly," I say casually.

"Wonderful."

"We just need to be careful. There is one thing I should note, though. The steel will still kill a demon; just make sure you strike a fatal blow on The Born, though. Otherwise, it'll only piss them off."

John stares at me blankly. Clearly, he would have preferred this information earlier in the day, but I may have been a bit distracted.

"Okay, good talk..." I say and continue walking.

John starts walking with me. "You really need to learn how to better explain things."

I just nod in agreement. He's probably right.

PUMPING STATION_
BETH

THIS PLACE HAS CHANGED DRASTICALLY SINCE I was here last. Granted, it has been more than a century. It just seems larger now.

When you walk through the station, it is wide open in the center with a clear view down to the main floor. Throughout the center are several large water pumps in an L-shape leading from the floor up to the walls, as well as straight pipes stretching from wall to wall. There are valves and caged rooms holding random circuit breakers scattered all around. We are standing on a ledge that wraps around the entire building. A single walkway stretches across the room. It ends in a stairwell that leads to the ledge on the floor below. It seems that each of the levels has a walkway like this. There are only three levels to get to the main floor. The room is damp and loud; you can hear the sound of the water rushing through the pipes. It's dark and I'm not sure what might be lurking around the corners.

As we stand at the ledge, John whispers. "Where do we go from here?"

"Wait, shh..."

That's when I heard the faint echoes of Steven and his friend in the distance. Luckily, through the sound of the water rushing through the pipes, I could still make out the location of where the echoing was coming from.

"I think I hear them. They must be on their way to the abandoned tunnels just outside the tomb — we must not be far behind them. We need to make our way down there."

I start across the walkway, taking each step lightly, trying to make as little noise as possible — John follows my lead. We make it to the end of the walkway and head down the stairs to the next level. Neither of us knowing what could be waiting for us.

We make it to the bottom of the stairs and as I turn to John to gesture which way to go next, two giant men sneak up on me. It's The Born.

"Beth!" John yells as I am hurled across the second sub-floor ledge. John follows shortly behind as the other one throws him like a ragdoll.

He hits the wall. "Son of a bitch... What is it with these guys and throwing people?"

I work on getting up while John is shaking off the

smack against the cement floor — we only have a second before The Born charge at us.

As there are only two of them, my plan is to use the same spell I used on the ones at John's apartment. Hoping this will launch them clear across the Pumping Station, injuring them, knocking them through the wall — fuck, I honestly do not know, I just need to get rid of them.

However, they were anticipating that. They begin charging before I could prepare my spell, but I try anyway.

I wasn't even entirely off the ground yet — one foot planted, one knee still on the ground — but I begin to raise my arms and speak. "INSPIR..." is all I can get out before I felt the full force of one of The Born charging me like a rhino charging its prey and I hit the floor once again.

John seems to be defenseless as the other one runs straight for him. I want to help, but I can't. The one who hit me watches with a sickening smile and a bit of laughter as if they have already won, and all I could do was watch it happen. The wind was knocked clean out of me and I lay on the floor just waiting for the air to rush back into my lungs. All I want to do is yell John's name to warn him, but I couldn't speak.

I watch as he is still on his knees with his head hung low as a force that he is not expecting barrels toward him. At that moment, I thought I was just forced to watch him die. No... John has something else up his sleeve.

He must have taken note that my direct approach did not work. The Born are fast on their feet, but once they get moving, there isn't much for a course correction, and I'm assuming John had picked up on that from his last encounter with them.

As John's would-be attacker is sprinting toward him, John is still on his knees, looking defeated — an easy target. However, as The Born neared, John quickly reaches over his right shoulder and grips the ivory handle of his grandfather's sword, and in one fluid motion, he unsheathes the blade and make a clean slice down The Born's torso.

When the blade makes contact with the skin of The Born, all that can be heard was the sound of blazing hot steel against The Born's skin — it's the char marks of the blade. The pure and raw energy of the Hellfire that it was forged in, still powering the magic that can kill these beasts. When it touches a demon or Fallen Angel, it burns through the skin, leaving a lasting mark.

Unfortunately, John did not cut far enough through The Born — instead, he only angered him, just as I said he would. The echo of the hot steal against The Born's skin made his attacker stumble and lose his focus. The one that had attacked me wiped his disgusting smile from his face. His jaw dropped at the sight of the blood from the scar on his brother's chest.

"Hellfire Forged?" My attacker asks John's in a deep gravel filled voice.

"You're Goddamn right it is..." John's attacker replies in apparent agony from the pain that he now feels.

The pain he is in caused a long enough pause for me to gain my strength back, and for John and me to refocus our fight.

I quickly shot up from the ground, and my attacker turned toward me and with an attempt to reach for my swords. I know exactly what he wants, but it is not my time. I have come too far, and I can almost smell the tomb from here. I am not going to die tonight — not by these bastards. I must at least get to Steven first.

John is still on his knees as his attacker is now enraged from the gash on his chest. John tries to jab his sword upward into The Born's chest, but it's knocked from his hand. The Born reaches down to grab John by the shirt to lift him in the air when John evades him, slides between his legs, and ends up behind him.

I jump up onto the back of my attacker and tie up his arm, hoping to pry it from its socket, but I know there is only one real way out of this. I reach for my Wakizashi blade and plunge it into the chest of The

Born. The scorch of his skin echoes as he drops to his knees.

John pulls his gun, but I call out to stop him. We've drawn too much attention to ourselves already. We can't let Steven, his friend, or anything else that might be here know we're just wandering around.

As his sword is out of reach, I pull mine from my attacker's chest and toss it to John. He catches it, spins it to face outward, and plunges it in the back of The Born, throwing all his body weight into it so it will puncture his heart. John will not make the 'non-fatal blow' mistake twice.

As both The Born are now dead, we fall to the floor and take a much-needed breath. I just want to say that again... Both The Born are dead... Holy shit, that was not an easy task. I mean, between you and me, because I would *not* say this to John since it will only upset him, I was expecting to die horribly if we ran into The Born tonight. I have to say, John is really showing a knack for this kind of work. I think we can make a real demon hunter out of him yet!

We're both still on the floor — both of us have our arms spread out as we gasp for any amount of air we can get. This has already been an eventful night and we've only just begun.

John turns his head and looks at me. "Thanks for the assist with your blade — that was pretty badass." He takes a deep breath and chuckles lightly. "You just keep saving my life."

I begin to stand up. "Well, John, I told you when we first met — I'm here to protect you."

He just smiles at me.

"I'll try to repay the favor one of these days." He winks, then slowly begins to stand up and joins me at my side. "Alright, well, we should get a move on."

"Yea, let's go!" I say as we begin heading for the next stairwell to take us deeper into the Pumping Station.

BETH'S TUNNEL VISION_
BETH

WE'RE FINALLY AT THE WATER TOWER PUMPING Station's ground floor and we enter the abandoned tunnel system. We follow the faint voices, which we can make out to be Steven and his friend, to a small doorway.

The doorway is an old steel door. It's smaller than an average door; it's rust-covered and would be easily overlooked as the entrance to a boiler room if you didn't know what to look for. It's slightly cracked open and we can better hear the two of them speaking.

"This is ridiculous. What the hell is taking you so long?" Steven asks to The Young Man.

"Seriously? I'm getting sick and tired of your fucking attitude," The Young Man responds.

I gesture to John that we should move in. Who

knows how far along they've come on the spell. We fought with The Born for a while. We've wasted enough time already.

We creep inside the abandoned tunnels. About fifty feet from the door, there is a fork that leads to more tunnels; they stretch throughout the city - it's a labyrinth in which one can easily be lost. To a mortal, one side of the tunnel system seems to be covered with rubble. That was an elaborate ploy I built up in 1871. Only demons and Fallen Angels can see the actual tomb door. The doorway is faint, but it's there, hidden within the brick wall. Behind that wall is the evil that The Watchers have been waiting to release since the day I locked them away.

We slowly step further into the tunnels and I can see what spell they are preparing. It's similar to the spell I prepared to unlock the armory - a blood spell. I'm not sure how they plan to use it though. Steven was not a witch before becoming a Tormented Demon — his friend must have powers like mine. So, unless Azazel intends to fly down here at the last second, I don't expect much from them, but we still need to be careful.

As we get a bit closer, I yell to Steven to distract them from their progress.

"Steven!"

Steven turns around in shock, and once he gets a glimpse of my face, it's utter disappointment.

"Son of a bitch... I take it our friends upstairs didn't make it," Steven says. "Can't you just take a hint and go fuck yourself?"

I ignore his comment.

"Steven, what happened to you?"

He faces me as if what he has to say next, he wants me to feel and have to suffer from.

"Your new boyfriend happened to me. Or should I say you both happened to me... When he arrested me that day, I couldn't get out of town." He glares at John and then continues, "Because of that, Azazel caught me and sent me back to Hell for reconditioning. You gotta love the Angel way down. I mean, I would have preferred to use the Hellgate — it's a lot less painful. But it's better this way. You had me in the field for so long." Steven begins to briefly show sorrow. "I was on my own because you were too afraid to be out in the world."

He's right. I left him out there for years, searching for every Obol he could get his hands on. We knew it was the best chance to keep The Watchers from prying this tomb open. If they got their hands on smart and mighty enough demons, they could find the blueprints to this place and a strong enough spell to open it. I also knew I couldn't risk being captured.

I didn't know what else to say except the truth. The truth is, what he is now is not better than what he was then.

"It's not..." I say with sadness. I know those two words won't get through to him, but they still needed to be said.

"Oh, but it is!" He says with excitement. "It's not like the good old days, Beth. We aren't partners anymore."

John's eyes widen. "Wait, you two used to work together?"

"Oh, yea!" Steven scoffs. "In fact, I knew your Great-Great-Great-Grandpappy," he says in a sarcastic southern drawl just to be a dick.

The Young Man decides to jump in, "My god, don't you know anything?"

John looks to me for answers, and I completely understand why. When he first met me, I promised to tell him everything. Now, the same person who caused him to find out the truth about the world is telling him that I held back a large part of his past, and mine... I just didn't want to hurt him. I just need to be honest.

"I didn't tell you because I had already piled so much on you. Steven used to be on my side — on our side. I tasked him with stealing the Obols, which led him to be sent back to Hell. It was my fault. All of this is my fault."

Everything is my fault. I genuinely don't know what else to say. If I had done a better job in 1871, the power of The Horsemen would be contained. If I had just gone after the Obols myself, Steven wouldn't have been captured and forced to recondition, and we wouldn't be here today. John would be safe, and he would still have Walter in his life.

Steven smiles at John. "I bet there's a lot she hasn't told you. Oh, here's a good one! All the missing people you've been investigating — yea, those were all demons disguised as humans all along." Steven laughs.

John is in disbelief.

"You didn't think it was strange that not one of them had a back story?" The Young Man chimes in with a bit of condescension in his voice.

John peers at The Young Man, then to Steven, then he gazes at me. He's disappointed and I feel terrible. I know exactly how long he spent on those cases because I was there keeping an eye on him the entire time. I wanted so badly to tell him it was pointless, but what was I to say? 'Oh, hey John, you don't know me, but don't worry about those missing people because they aren't really people after all?' Yea... that would have gone over well.

I knew he would have never believed a word I had to say unless he saw it firsthand. I wouldn't feel so bad if these cases didn't cause his partner and his — for lack of a better word — father to go missing. I just need him to understand why I didn't tell him.

Those eyes... In The Vault, John's eyes said

everything. His eyes were full of strength and hope. Now, they just show me anger and fear. That's my fault — I never wanted that... Goddammit, it's all my fault.

"They were all—?" John begins to ask but was interrupted by Steven.

"Demons? Yup!" Steven responds before I could get a chance to.

Steven looks at me, knowing him answering before me would only further upset John.

"You see, we... we as in me and your little girlie here... we gave them just enough personal information to get by." Steven continues on as I stood silent. I didn't know what to say. "You see, they were sent to stop all of this from happening! But just like with me, Azazel got to them first. Reconditioning... it's a bitch — but it works!"

I had to jump in. "John, I swear I was going to tell you every—"

"Just don't..." John cut me off.

John is staring at the floor. I just want him to look at me. I want to tell him to look in my eyes like he did back at my place. He'll know I didn't mean to hurt him if he just looks in my eyes. I know he felt something, and I know he can trust me. He just needs to look at me.

The Young Man is leaning against the tunnel wall, giggling. "Oh boy... trouble in paradise already."

"Fuck off," John says without breaking eye contact with the floor.

"Aw, I'm hurt," The Young Man responds.

Steven chimes in, "Come on, John, you're smarter than that. You had to know something crazy was going on with those cases!"

"Well, yea, of course," John says. "Walter and I were about to look into them before he disappeared."

The Young Man chuckles again. "And now you never can..."

"Seriously, fuck off," John says, but this time peering directly at him.

The Young Man put his hands up to gesture 'alright...' submissively, but sarcastically.

John finally looks my way. I should have been more careful what I wished for. This was not the look I had been getting from him all night. His eyes were different. It was like he doesn't even know me. What am I saying — he doesn't know me. After years of being alone and working from the shadows, I've never owed the entire truth to anyone. Yes, the people John and Walter were searching for were all my people, but I didn't owe them the entire truth. I mourned their losses and moved on. In this business, we all know what we sign up for. Take Steven for example — he was one of the first to join my team, but at this moment, I will not hesitate to kill him myself if it comes to that. Because that's who I am. Maybe it makes me a bad person and maybe that's why I was so set on pulling away from John in The Vault earlier. He doesn't deserve the ice that has grown over my heart in the last century... or maybe he can be the one to melt it. I see the betrayal in his eyes, it begins to destroy me. I can only imagine what he might be thinking.

JOHN'S TUNNEL VISION_
JOHN

SON OF A BITCH... I AM READY TO CUT OUT THIS fucking guy's heart.

Steven is just stirring the pot, but for some reason, I'm letting him do it. Dammit, John, pull it together.

But his friend... He just sits back and lobs in a comment here, a 'dead Walter' jab there. Just enough to really piss me off. Who the fuck does he think he is? I mean, I don't even know the guy, he thinks he can just barge in on my life?

I'm usually not so temperamental, but it tends to mess with you when the first person you trust after spending nearly two years of building walls lies to your face.

Is it wrong to say that I don't want to look at her? Not because I'm upset, but because I don't want her to be bothered that she upset me? Maybe that's a sign of how I'm really feeling right now.

I take my eyes off the floor for the first time and look at her for a second, then I speak. I try to mask my true feelings — honestly, I think I'm doing a pretty good job...

Beth looks devastated — I think I'm doing a worse job hiding my feelings than I thought.

"Why didn't you tell me they were your people?" That's when I realize something. "Wait, if you knew they were going missing, you had to have known about the cases Walter and I had. Which means you knew about me but never approached me. So, how much more is there that you haven't told me?"

I was fighting myself from speaking the words because I didn't want to know the answer. I didn't want to know that there could be so much more to this ludicrous story. I didn't want to think that she was hiding something or that she might not be entirely on my side, or on the right side, after all. However, the words came out anyway, and Beth responded.

"With everything going on already, I didn't think it was the time to drop that on you." I can sense hesitation in her voice. "I mean, I was the reason you weren't able to solve those cases. And Walter... To be honest, I felt responsible for his disappearance. If not for me, you wouldn't be in this mess." She takes a deep breath. "That's why I didn't approach you sooner. First of all, would you have believed me if you didn't see it for yourself? And even if you did, it would have only put you in danger sooner."

She's right. The second I learned the truth it was death and destruction all around. This is by no means Beth's fault; you can't really avoid demons once you know they are out there.

That's when Steven decides it's his turn to weigh in.

"Well Johnny Boy, you have your culprit! You've been looking for the responsible party, and she just owned up to it! And there's only one way for you to get even — kill the bitch! Isn't that what you've been searching for the last two years? Revenge? Revenge on the person who took Walter from you?"

Beth, who is not sure where I stand at this moment mentally or emotionally, was thrown off by Steven's call for revenge on her. She took a large step back and places a hand on her Katana handle just in case.

"No!" I shout. "Enough. I'm not going to let you get in my head anymore. She didn't tell me what was going on, but she had her reasons, and I'm okay with that."

I turn to Beth and she slowly lowers her hand from her blade. She smiles at me — a quick thank you.

Steven chimes in as The Young Man paces with impatience behind him. "Oh fine, it was worth a shot... It's really touching to see you lovebirds make up and all, but if you don't mind getting a room, we have work to do."

Beth steps forward and stands her ground.

"Not going to happen. I can't sit back and watch as you open the tomb. You know damn well what this will bring. Besides, I don't know how you plan on getting this thing open — you'd be lucky enough to even get one of The Horsemen out of there."

"One is all we need, Beth, you know that." The Young Man says. "And don't worry about how. We have it all under control."

I could see the rage coming from Beth. I think she hates Steven's friend just as much as I do. I mean, honestly, who the hell does he think he is?

Beth decides it's best to ignore him and try once more to pull the best part of Steven out of him.

"Steven, please, this isn't you. You know exactly what will happen if you let them win. You stood side by side with me for years. Don't let that all go to waste now..."

Beth's plea seems to have been getting through. The silence in the tunnel was almost uncomfortable and we wait for Steven to snap out of the funk he has been in. The look on his face shows that he is fighting hard to break from the reconditioning.

As we wait for him to say anything, hoping that it would end with him turning on his friend, The Young Man speaks up.

"AH! Can we *please* just fucking kill them already?"

The look on Steven's face changes drastically. He was no longer in the contemplative state he was in. The face Beth and I both wished was saying he would make the right choice in the end was gone. Instead, he slowly turned to The Young Man and says, "Eh, why not?"

"Finally..." The Young Man responds in a calm and menacing tone.

The Young Man raises his arm in the air, and I feel as if everything around me begins to slow down all over again. I could see the faint red color start to glow in his eyes as he telekinetically lifts me off the ground — the exact same way he did when we were at Steven's apartment the night before.

"Hmm... familiar," The Young Man says with a smirk on his face. He is now holding me in the air without touching me, but I could feel the force against my throat and the air draining from my lungs.

"No!" Beth yells out as The Young Man hoists me into the air.

Beth and I are standing next to each other, but at this point, I am looking down on her. I can't begin to explain why time seems to freeze... maybe it's the adrenaline, maybe it's the magic in the air — or perhaps I am just slowly dying from strangulation. However, looking down at Beth as she draws her weapons makes her look like a God damn superhero.

That's when I realize I am losing more oxygen than I should be because I could swear she is wearing a cape...

Beth draws both of her blades simultaneously and charges The Young Man, but Steven steps in. She spins out from Steven's way, knocking him to the side. At full speed, Beth continues toward The Young Man, intending to ram both blades into his ribs. That's when he drops me to the ground and holds one hand up toward Beth. He smiles as he stops her on a dime. Her speed and the impact of the energy he uses against her slams Beth to the floor. Both her blades slide from her grip.

I'm now on the floor gasping for air but I know it's only a matter of seconds before I need to join the fight. Steven, who was able to keep his balance after Beth shoulder-checked him like an old school, goon-style hockey player, is now taking aim at me while Beth and The Young Man duke it out.

Steven charges toward me, as I am still kneeling over trying to catching my breath — what a way to fight fair. Once he gets close and thinks he has a shot against me, I duck my head and shoulder and flip him over my back.

Steven lands hard on the floor behind me, and in one motion, I spin around, pull my sword from behind my back, and attempt to plunge it into his chest. It's time to end this — but Steven dives out of the way. However, he is not as fast as he thinks. I may not have hit the target I was hoping to, but I was able to slice part of his arm as he moved his body out of the way.

As the blade slices clean through his skin, Steven could feel the heat from the Hellfire Forged Steel, and a striking realization fell over his face. The sound of hot steel could be heard and, for a moment, he was terrified.

Unfortunately, I became a bit too cocky with the sight of his fear, allowing him to get the upper hand on me. He knocks my blade from my hand, grabs my wrist, and flips me. I am now stuck on my back.

Steven took this time to let his friend know just what they were up against.

"The steel!" Steven yells.

The Young Man who has been locked in a telekinetic and spell-wielding dual with Beth, each blow more powerful than the last, takes a second to gaze at Beth's blades lying on the floor near them. He can now see the char marks lining the edge of both blades.

The Young Man, with a menacing smile, looks to Beth. "Oh, you're good..."

The Young Man lunges for one of Beth's blades. Knowing exactly what he wants, Beth jumps for them as well. They struggle for control. This will settle everything. She knows that Steven could not break the spell. He has no witchcraft, only demonic gifts — it needs to be The Young Man. He could not walk out of here today.

While they struggle, I continue to fight with Steven. Steven may not have the same telekinetic gifts as his friend, which may lead you to believe the playing field is a bit more level, but he is much stronger than I am. Holding him back from literally beating me to death is not an easy task.

However, during my fight, I can see that The Young Man begins to overpower Beth. She, too, is on her back, except she now has a blade hanging over her chest. A blade made from the same steel that can kill her if she is struck with it.

What am I to do? I see this and a white-hot rage fills within me. I know I need to help her, but I need to get Steven off me so I can get to her.

All I can see is Beth fighting. And again, my vision slows, but I cannot understand why. Maybe it's just the adrenaline... or is it because I know I stand on the precipice of certain death if the right move is not made? Even worse, is it because Beth will most likely die if I cannot strengthen up and do what I need to.

I look over at Beth one last time. I can tell she can't hold out any longer.

"No! Beth!" I say, knowing that won't do anything, but the words fall out of my mouth anyway. Seeing Beth near-death strikes fear in my heart — I don't know what to do. That's when I remember I have one more trick up my sleeve.

I find a way to kick Steven back just enough to give myself room to grab my gun from the holster on my hip.

I draw my gun and fire two rounds, striking Steven once in the stomach and again in the chest. The sound of hot steel against his flesh is flushed out this time by the gunshot echoing throughout the tunnel. I hear it, though, and Steven feels the pain as the energy courses through him.

He stands tall for the last time. Then, he begins to stagger. I immediately point my gun at The Young Man with the intention of firing, but there is no need. The Young Man has already backed away from Beth and he held the sword, with which he was planning to kill Beth just seconds ago, loosely.

"What have you done?" The Young Man says in shock as he finally drops Beth's blade to the ground.

Pools of blood form on Steven's torso as he finally drops to the ground. He lies flat on his back for the three of us to see. The Young Man has no doubt in his mind, if there ever was one, that he's next.

The second Steven's body hit the floor, The Young Man sprints to the tunnel door and is gone. I guess the spell to open the tomb wasn't that much of a concern to him any longer.

I rush to Beth's side and wrap my arms around her. I do it out of instinct, but then I realize I can't let her go. Her hair is in her face, so I carefully brush it away.

"Are you okay?" I ask.

Beth places her hand on my back.

"I'm fine. Are you?" she responds.

As we hold onto each other, we pull our heads apart and stare, just a bit too long. I want to kiss her, and I swear she wants to kiss me. I just can't bring myself to make the first move.

"Yea, I'm fine," I answer.

I slowly let her go, as much as I hate myself for it.

I gesture to Steven. "I'm sorry about your friend."

"He hasn't been a friend of mine for a long time," Beth says with a bit of sadness in her voice.

That's when I knew it was time to break the tension.

"Well, on the bright side, at least we stopped them!" I say, feeling as if we actually did something good.

Beth smiles, only for a moment.

"Yes and no..." Beth hesitates. "We stopped them from opening the tomb, but the power of The Horsemen is still getting out. We can still see it today with all the divisions in everyday life. Eventually, The Watchers will try to reopen this tomb. Steven and his friend were just the beginning."

My feeling of accomplishment fades quickly. I was now feeling the sense of fear I had when Beth found me in Steven's apartment last night...

"So, now what? All of this was for nothing?" I ask, feeling a bit defeated.

"No, of course not!" She takes a breath. "The 'now what' is up to you. You know what's out there in the world now, so it might be a bit hard to go back to your everyday life. And I have a friend that can help us seal this tomb a bit tighter to keep the powers locked in. So, you can either go back to the old John or you can come fight the good fight with me." Beth smiles.

"I don't know. Now that I know more about what could have happened to Walter, I feel like I have a real chance of finding him."

"I understand," Beth says but doesn't seem happy.

"But... that doesn't mean I can't work with you in the process!" I wink as I continue on.

"That works for me!" Beth says with a smile.

"Now that I think about it, didn't you blow up my apartment?"

"Oh, yea... about that..." Beth trails off.

"I think I might need a place to stay for a bit. You wouldn't be looking for a temporary roommate, would you?" I ask, but in a way to let her know she owes me one.

"Yea, I think I have a spare room for you... Come on, let's go home, roomie!

THE TOMB_

THE ABANDONED TUNNELS BENEATH THE WATER Tower Pumping Station are cold, dark, and damp. For the very few employees that venture down there, they occasionally come across the collapsed tunnel.

These tunnels were originally built in 1864, so a collapsed tunnel found this close to the Water Tower Pumping Station door is not entirely out of the question. However, it's the feeling that it gives mortals each time they are forced to pass by that's particularly interesting. It's a chill that runs down your spine. The same one that makes anyone detest being in the tunnels for too long.

In 1871, a spell was created to lock in place The Four Horsemen of the Apocalypse and their Champion — The Anti-Christ. In doing so, a doorway was created. It was an unfortunate part of the spell. You see, all magic has a give and take. I guess you can say nothing can be lost forever. So, to keep this hidden from prying eyes, a second spell was placed over the rock wall. To a mortal's eyes, it appears to be nothing more than rubble. That's both great and terrible news.

The great news, the tomb contains the physical forms of the evil within. They cannot get out. And for all those who truly cannot comprehend what they seek, they will never find what they are searching for.

You see, humanity... well, it's fickle. At any given moment, we can be the best or the worst. You may have known someone when you were just a child that grew up to accomplish wondrous things. However, on the other hand, you may have known someone that grew up to be a total piece of shit. Sorry, but I'm not known for beating around the bush.

To be honest, you may be either one of those people — who am I to judge if you become the latter? Asshole... Again, I like the direct approach.

Now, the terrible news, those who can see the doorway are searching for it. And they can comprehend what they seek.

It's the give and take...

They want, not only, for the evil within to be released, but for the God-awful villains that live among us, already capable of unspeakable things, to be influenced by their untold power.

That... well, that is where we fall tonight.

Just hours after Beth and John left the Water

Tower Pumping Station, the starry-eyed duo, who thought they had just conquered all, head back to Beth's apartment for a long-overdue night's rest. However, the events in the abandoned tunnels just outside the rubble were far from over.

The spell that Steven and The Young Man set still lie in place, half prepared and scattered around the area. At the moment, there are only bits that are finished.

A man enters the tunnel. He walks past a small table that The Young Man had originally placed all the other necessary ingredients for the spell on before Beth and John disturbed him and Steven.

The man approaches the table, he picks up a small bowl of incense and walks toward the most significant piece to this entire spell. Which is on the floor just a few feet from where the door should be.

He kneels down and places the bowl on the floor next to it.

The man begins to speak. "Steven, my old friend..." The man places his hand on Steven's chest.

The main piece to the spell — the body of a Tormented Demon that lies dead on his back with two bullet holes from Hellfire Forged Steel rounds.

Steven James is that Tormented Demon, sent to Hell on Azazel's orders to be reconditioned to open the tomb, now dead as the sacrifice.

The man continues on, "It's Armers. I know you can't hear me, but wherever you are now, I hope you understand why we couldn't tell you our plans for you."

The man in the tunnels is Chief Armers. The same man who forced John to retire from the Chicago Police Department, who caused Ben to go into hiding, and who may very well be involved with the disappearance of John's mother.

Armers looks away from Steven while fighting back a tear. Steven's loss is a bittersweet feeling for Armers. For a moment, you feel his grief. He cared for Steven, and this loss begins to eat at him. But only for a moment.

Armers looks back at Steven once more. "It's a shame you won't see the glory unfold. But I will hold your memory close, knowing your death brought us our victory."

Then, with a smile, Armers moves onto the next phase.

He lifts Steven's arm from the ground and holds it over the bowl of incense next to him. With a wave of his hand, a large incision runs from Steven's elbow to his wrist and blood drips down his arm and off his fingers onto the incense below.

Armers stands up and places the bowl of incense just a couple of feet from the front of the tomb wall. He then takes a piece of chalk and draws two 7-pointed stars, one of which is directly in front of the wall with the bowl of incense in the center. The other is on the wall of the tomb, where the door would be. Then, he places one candle on each point of the star on the floor. Lastly, he waves his hand over the incense bowl, and black smoke begins to pour out.

Armers takes a step back, stands over Steven's lifeless body, and begins the spell. A spell that he speaks in Latin. However, I will do my best to translate for you.

"To call out The Champion and The First Four Seals, I call on The Spirits, The Saints, The Martyrs, The Beasts."

The flames on the candles set, and both stars begin to glow with a golden light. For a split second, the door on the tomb is visible to the naked eye.

Armers repeats the spell again.

"To call out The Champion and The First Four Seals, I call on The Spirits, The Saints, The Martyrs, The Beasts."

The black smoke turns blood-red and billows around the room, then settles around Steven's body. Both chalk outlines are now flashing with a bright golden glow. It's nearly blinding. The tomb door is now completely visible to anyone, and the spell that keeps The Horsemen entombed is breaking down.

At that moment, wings burst from Armers' shoulders through his police uniform. He already stands at a staggering 6.5 feet tall and what seems to be 250 pounds of pure muscle. When you add in his feathered and pale red wings, it's truly terrifying. They match Azazel's wings exactly, down to the strange branding and all, which could only mean one thing: Chief Armers is not just a magical being. No, in fact, he is one of The Watchers that Beth has lost track of after all these years.

Now, with his wings out, he is even more powerful. He can pull energy from them. So, he repeats the spell one last time.

"To call out The Champion and The First Four Seals, I call on The Spirits, The Saints, The Martyrs, The Beasts."

The candles erupt in flames, the light from both stars are now engulfing the room. Suddenly, it all comes to a halt. The blood-red smoke from the incense begins to dissipate. The smoke, which covered Steven's body completely, is now being absorbed into the tomb wall. However, with the disappearance of the smoke, Steven's body has also gone missing. There is absolutely no trace of him. Not even a single drop of blood. However, Armers does not seem to notice. Instead, he looks around for a sign that the spell has worked.

That's when he hears a noise. It's a crack from the tomb. The rubble shifts and the door begins to slowly swing open.

From behind the door, a century's worth of dust rolls out. With it, two figures appear.

The Champion.

The First Rider.

Dear reader,

We hope you enjoyed reading *The Tomb*. Please take a moment to leave a review, even if it's a short one. Your opinion is important to us.

Discover more books by Carl Novakovich at https://www.nextchapter.pub/authors/carl-novakovich

Want to know when one of our books is free or discounted? Join the newsletter at http://eepurl.com/bqqB3H

Best regards,

Carl Novakovich and the Next Chapter Team

The Tomb
ISBN: 978-4-82410-122-8
Large Print

Published by
Next Chapter
1-60-20 Minami-Otsuka
170-0005 Toshima-Ku, Tokyo
+818035793528

25th August 2021

Lightning Source UK Ltd.
Milton Keynes UK
UKHW012141170921
390772UK00001B/105